AMISH
PROMISE

A Sequel to Amish Dilemma

A Novel by

SIOUX DALLAS

CCB Publishing
British Columbia, Canada

Amish Promise: A Sequel to Amish Dilemma

Copyright ©2013 by Sioux Dallas
ISBN-13   978-1-77143-050-0
First Edition

Library and Archives Canada Cataloguing in Publication

Dallas, Sioux, 1930-
Amish promise : a sequel to Amish dilemma / written by Sioux Dallas. – 1st ed.
ISBN 978-1-77143-050-0
Also available in electronic format.
Additional cataloguing data available from Library and Archives Canada

Disclaimer: This is a book of pure fiction, a product of the author's imagination, and does not represent any person, living or dead.

Extreme care has been taken by the author to ensure that all information presented in this book is accurate and up to date at the time of publishing. Neither the author nor the publisher can be held responsible for any errors or omissions. Additionally, neither is any liability assumed for damages resulting from the use of the information contained herein.

Publisher: CCB Publishing
             British Columbia, Canada
             www.ccbpublishing.com

Dedicated to Bonnie Kaye, whom I have learned to love even though we have never met. Bonnie has a heart of gold and is concerned about everyone. She has dedicated her life to being helpful and making life more pleasant and satisfying for others.

BOOKS WRITTEN BY SIOUX DALLAS

First Experience

Sharon

Desperate Wish

L i i s a

Death in Three Quarter Time

The Perfect Spouse

Montana Madness

Dangerous Hilarity

Amish Dilemma

A Detective's Heart

Amish Promise

And coming soon:

The Snowman Murders

Streets of Laredo (a paranormal)

Be anxious for nothing, but in everything by

prayer and supplication, with thanksgiving.

Let your requests be made known to God

and the peace of God, which surpasses all

understanding, will guard your hearts and

minds through Christ Jesus.

Philippians 4: 6-7

PREFACE

If you read my novel *Amish Dilemma*, you learned a lot about the truth of the Amish and their beliefs. You learned how passive and forgiving they are and hard working.

Of course they are human just like any other people. A few bad ones can be found in the group, but they are generally taken care of, by the church, as soon as they are discovered. They punish their own.

In *Amish Dilemma* I wrote of a young couple who married, not for love, but because their families expected it. They quickly became very much in love and adored each other. They worked hard to make a home and to be good church members and good neighbors.

When the young woman, Charity, was in labor with their first baby, her husband, Adam Kime, was taking her to the hospital in a horse-drawn buggy. An English (one not an Amish) was drinking and hated the Amish. He deliberately ran his car toward the horse, honking his horn and yelling. The horse jumped, out of fright, and the car hit the side of the buggy. The horse, which the young couple loved dearly, was injured so badly she had to be put down. The young husband was killed and the young mother gave birth to a healthy boy on the same night her husband was killed.

Charity named the little boy Jeremiah.

Her father, Jacob Startz, and her father-in-law, Joshua Kime bought a building in town to give to Charity because they knew Charity was too proud to accept help. They convinced her to open a store where she became well known for her integrity and industriousness. Even English began to trade with her and loved her. Some of her relatives and friends volunteered to help.

Charity was successful and, even though she was a nineteen year old widow and mother, she worked hard and planned ahead.

This story follows *Amish Dilemma*. I hope you enjoy it as much as you did *Amish Dilemma*. I am forever grateful for your wonderful comments and encouragement.

God bless you all.

CHAPTER ONE

The bare feet of six-year-old Jeremiah Kime slapped happily on the rich, fertile farm land as he ran to tell his mother the good news.

He hoped his mamm, Charity, was still at the house so he could share his good news. Grossmudder Kime had made a banana pie especially for him. Grossfader Startz had told him he was now big enough to help in the field.

"Mamm! Mamm!" he yelled, running into the kitchen door. Charity came running thinking something terrible had happened to her beloved son. (Mamm - Mom)

"What? What's wrong?" she asked breathlessly.

"Nuttins wrong. It is all so good."

"The word is nothing and what is so good?" she sat down relieved.

"Grossfader Startz said I am now big enough to ride with him on the cutter behind the mules. I get to work in the fields with him." He paused to take a breath. "And Grossmudder Kime made a banana pie specially for me." He strutted around.

"I hope you remembered to thank Grandfather Startz for being willing to allow you to work for him; and Grandmother Kime for baking your favorite pie."

"I did. Yes, I did." *I hope I did. I don't remember. I was too happy.*

Charity stooped to hug him again. She did love this little son of hers so much. He had Adam's blood in him, too and she would always love Adam. Jeremiah was a daily reminder of Adam.

"I am so proud of you. Of course you're big enough to work now. You'll have to wear your shoes though because you might step on a snake. You wouldn't want those big mules to accidentally step on your bare feet either."

"No," he said solemnly, "I don't want any of that. See you, Mamm. I'm going to tell Oom Matthew." He ran out the kitchen door when he saw his mother's brother riding the tractor and working in the field. He loved his uncle Matthew.

"Don't slam the door and don't get in the way of the tractor." Charity called after him. She smiled and shook her head. Too late. He was too excited to notice what he was doing. She just hoped Matthew would see him before he stepped in front of the tractor. She ran to the door and breathed a sigh of relief when she saw Matthew pause to lift Jeremiah on the tractor with him.

She took advantage of the tractor motor being off. "Matthew, Matthew." He looked in her direction and waved his hat. "It is almost eight and I have to go open the store. Can you keep an eye on Jeremiah? If you have to do something else, take him to our parents, please."

He waved his hat and nodded that he understood. She quickly hitched a horse to a buggy and started off to work. Kyle Snyder would be in later to bring the horse back home so that he wouldn't have to stand in the heat all day. Christine and Ruth Ann, the Zook twins, were coming in to help quilt. Lisa Kennedy had asked if she could just volunteer to do whatever Charity needed doing.

The work in the store and the demands were more than her little store could manage now. She was pleasantly surprised because she had never thought she would do this well.

Jacob and Joshua had been discussing the increase in her business. They had made plans to buy the land beside her and add a couple of rooms. Several English women had been in hoping to find clothing for themselves.

Charity was lost in thought as she worked. *Jeremiah will be in school this fall and I would like to sell clothing to the English. Enough of them come in to shop and visit. I am grateful for their business, but I do need to expand. I have an idea I am going to discuss with daed.*

That night, Jacob came to make his nightly visit and see if she needed anything. She was surprised when he was joined by Joshua. Her mamm, Jenna Mae, and mamm-in-law, Leah, soon came bringing pies and homemade cider.

Charity was mystified as to why they all came, but she knew it would be bad manners to ask.

After pie and coffee they all settled around the kitchen table for a second cup of coffee and to talk.

"Well, dochder, wie geht's?" (Daughter, how are you?)

"I'm fine, danki."

"Gut. We'd like to discuss something with you. Since you do not have a husband to take care of you, we are happy to do so. Joshua and I went ahead and purchased the acre next to your store. That old building on it will have to come down and we would like to add two or three rooms to your store. Your business is growing more than any of us realized it would. You will have to be hiring some help before long.

Your quilting frame is up in the storeroom and is crowded. One of the rooms could be just for sewing. The quilting frame could be set up and left up and people could come in and sew."

Charity was so engrossed in hearing her father's voice, as he rarely talked that much at one time, that she barely took in what he was saying. She loved hearing his deep rumble.

Jenna Mae, Charity's mother spoke up. "We are all willing to help you with Jeremiah and anything you need. We will be there to sew for you, too."

"Nee. I could not ask you to do that. If you did sew, I would pay you like anyone else." She realized what they were saying.

Her mother-in-law spoke. "Charity, it is a blessing to us to help you. I love to quilt and we have many women in the church who will be delighted to help quilt."

"I know and you are one of the best quilters I have seen, but ---"

"But nothing," Joshua spoke, "Jeremiah is my grandson, too and you are still my daughter-in-law. That makes you my child, too. I want to do what is best for you. At this time you need more room and Jacob and I are going to see that you get it."

Charity knew they spoke the truth and she was touched and grateful that they wanted to help. Her independent streak came out and she declared, "I hate to be a burden forever on all of you. I need to take care of myself and provide for Jeremiah."

"Adam would be so proud of you," his mother, Leah, spoke with a smile. "We all are. You have worked hard to keep house, put out a garden, work in your store and take care of your precious gift from God, your son. We love you and want, no, we insist on helping you. It is not a burden to us."

Her mother quickly agreed. "Several of the women in church have commented on you and their pride in you. There will be many willing hands when you get the frame up and quilters can gather around it in comfort."

"I will think about it and I am grateful to everyone. I am glad you came tonight for I have been wanting to discuss something with you."

She turned to Jacob. "Daed, do you have cousins in Indiana? I am especially interested in Shipshewana, Indiana."

At that moment Matthew and Deborah walked in. Matthew laughed, "Mine schwesechder wants to go so far away from home when we are lucky to get her into the next town. What is up?"

"Your little sister knows what she is doing," Charity laughed and went to hug her beloved brother and sister-in-law."

"I was just telling everyone I want to go to Shipshewana to visit their big store where everything is sold. I would like to know how they manage, where they get their supplies, and ---- I am full of questions." She laughed.

"I think it is a gut idea," Matthew said smiling at Deborah.

"We will be glad to keep Jeremiah for you," Deborah said hopefully. Everyone loved the little boy. Matthew and Deborah had not yet had children and they were anxious.

"That is so gut of you and I do appreciate it. I am not worried about Jeremiah because I know there are many of you to take care of him. I just hate to leave him. We have never been apart."

"He will have a great time. I will teach him to use a bat and ball," Matthew assured her.

The next day being a Sunday with no service meant visiting or working on hobbies. Charity was reading a children's book with Jeremiah when she heard buggy wheels and the clop of a horse's hooves. Jeremiah had learned to read quickly and didn't want to give up his time with his mother whom he loved dearly and knew she loved him.

Charity was delighted to see Benjamin and Angela Lapp and their three boys. Jeremiah was delighted to see the boys and hurried outside to play with them.

Coffee was kept going in most Amish homes and Charity was no exception. She soon had coffee and pecan pie on the kitchen table where they sat to talk and relax.

They talked about Clint and Purity Kime expecting their first child and about the death of some older members. They spoke well of Moses Yoder as the Bishop and knew he was doing a good job.

Charity finally told them of her wish to go to Shipshewana and check out the big Yoder store there. They thought it was a great idea and offered to help any way they could while she was gone.

"Thank you so much, but I have a big family willing to help with the store, this farm and my precious son." she laughed. "They will have their hands full with Jeremiah."

At that moment the four boys ran in asking for cookies and lemonade. Angela poured drinks while Charity sat out three kinds of cookies; Amish walnut kisses, Whoopie cookies and Springerle. (The recipes for all of these can be found in *Amish Dilemma*)

The time passed too quickly and the Lapp family went home.

Charity took Jeremiah by the hand and walked across the field to her parents' home. They were just returning home from visiting other families. Jenna Mae insisted on getting nachtesse for everyone, so Charity stayed to help her mother and share a supper meal with them.

She told her family of her plans. "I have decided to go the first week of September because school will have started and Jeremiah will be busy most of the time. Rosemary and the Zook twins have agreed to mind the store and Rosemary can bring her baby with her."

"How will you travel, dochder?" Jacob questioned. "Do you need money?"

"Nee, daed, danki. I have money thanks to you and daed Joshua, I have a good bank balance. I will go by bus because it does not cost as much and it will go straight into Shipshewana."

"But you will get hungry," Jenna Mae said. "On the train you could sleep and eat."

"I will sleep all right on the bus and I will take food with me, at least enough to last until I get there. I feel comfortable that everything is covered. The train doesn't go close to there, but the bus does."

They talked until it was getting dark. Jacob walked them home. He hugged Charity and told her again how proud he was of her. He blew a raspberry in Jeremiah's neck and got him excited.

"Oh, I will have a time getting him settled for the night." Charity laughed.

She bathed Jeremiah and then read the Biewel to him. The Bible was important in every Amish home.

"Would my daed have read to me and tucked me in?" Jeremiah asked as he had many nights.

"Yes, mine lieb. He loved knowing you were on the way and could hardly wait to welcome you. It was a senseless and evil accident that took him away from us. He was on the way to meet you at the hospital and was excited to bring you home. He loved you then and I am sure he is so happy that you are such a good boy."

They went up to bed. She tucked Jeremiah in, listened to his prayer and kissed his cheek. "Sweet dreams, my little man."

She then did as she had many nights. She walked out and looked up at the stars. "Adam, I still love you so much. It has been a little over six years and I feel you would approve of all I have planned. By now we would have had more bopplis. It is Gottes wille and we are not supposed to understand, I guess." God's will was important to them.

"Gut nacht mine lieb," she whispered her usual good night.

CHAPTER TWO

Charity finally, and prayerfully, agreed to teach Lisa Kennedy how to keep her financial records. Lisa was so heart broken because her husband and his family had caused so much grief for Charity and the community. She wanted to prove she could be trusted and would be faithful to Charity, as well as never talking Charity's business in public.

She placed Rosemary as manager of the store and kept the willing workers they had. She knew Rosemary could be trusted.

Jeremiah could not comprehend that his mother would be gone for a short time. He had never spent a night away from her and had a lot of questions. Everyone, with whom he talked, assured him that he is loved and would be well cared for and his mother would return in a short time. He would stay with Matthew and Deborah, but would be free to go to other relatives homes as he did now. Besides school would start soon and he was too excited to contain his exuberance. He was a year later starting to school. His mother had already taught him to read and recognize some numbers, but he would at last be able to carry a lunch bucket and a backpack like the big kids did. His teacher would be Marilyn Kime, his Uncle Noah's frau.

School was such a wonderful, exciting experience. He had never been to a movie, never watched television, did not have the games that the Englisch children had and now he would be able to carry his lunch and study with other children. He planned what he would like to carry in his lunch.

Charity continued to prepare for her trip. She had never been on such a long trip, and alone. She made sure all of her helpers knew what to do in the store, and made Matthew crazy reminding him how to care for Jeremiah.

The time came closer and Jeremiah began begging to go with her. "Oh, precious. I need you to be the man of the house and keep an eye on our property. I will be back before you have time to miss me."

"But I already miss you, mamm."

She quoted Philippians 4:6-7 to him. "What does that mean, mamm?"

"It means we must have faith and trust God to take care of us."

"I do, mamm, and I will pray for you every night. You will come back to me won't you? I will not lose you like I did my daed."

"No, my darling. I'll be back to you soon and God will take care of both of us.

"Mamm, what will you put in my lunch that first day?"

"Oh, I don't know. Probably a big ham and egg sandwich with a cup of potato salad and one of jello. I'll also put in a bottle of milk and a big piece of cake. You must take care and bring the bottle back home to use again."

"What kind of cake, mamm?" he asked crawling in her lap and giving her a hug.

"I don't know yet. It is another week until the big day. I will fix something extra good for my little man. I know Deborah will fix a lot of good things for you, too."

"Will the other children like me? Will tante Marilyn like me as a student?"

"The other children will like you and treat you just as you treat them. Your tante Marilyn absolutely must be called Mrs. Kime in school. She must have respect and cooperation from all of you. Oom Matthew will still be Oom Matthew. He is your uncle and deserves respect. You must be polite and kind to everyone, especially adults."

"I will, mamm. I promise I will."

She hugged him to her with the thought that he would soon consider himself too big to sit in her lap and be hugged. She held him close and enjoyed the feeling.

Charity gathered the last of the vegetables out of the garden to cook and eat or to can. There were still some potatoes to dig. She was trying to remember to do a lot of things before time for her to leave. She made two pair of pants and two shirts for Jeremiah. These would be enough with his other clothes for school. He was growing so fast she knew she would soon be donating his clothes to another family with growing children.

She decided to bake cookies and cakes to take over to Deborah because she knew Jeremiah's sweet tooth -- Matthew's, also.

She mentally checked down a list to be sure someone would milk the cow and take care of the other animals. When she was satisfied that she had covered everything, she got her clothes, and food, ready for her trip.

She packed a green dress, a light blue one and a black one. Two aprons, two nightgowns, two pair of shoes and two prayer kapps followed. She had just finished making herself some new bloomers, so three pair went in the suitcase with three pairs of stockings she had made. Her Bible would be the last thing she packed. The suitcase had been a gift from an English friend.

Charity got a canvas bag from her hope chest to carry her food in. She would place the food in fresh tomorrow morning when she prepared to leave.

As usual, she was up by five thirty. She milked the cow and fed her, then fed the horses and turned them out in the pasture near the house. The chickens were fed and the eggs gathered. She slopped the hogs and then went in to get breakfast for Jeremiah and herself.

Jeremiah was excited. This was his second day of school and he loved it. He felt a little sad that his mamm was leaving, but he knew she would be back soon. He loved his oom Matthew and tante Deborah and knew he would enjoy living with them. Besides the Grossdawdis would be close and ready to help at any time.

Jeremiah was excited and wanted to help his mamm pack her food while she packed his lunch. He asked for a homemade peanut butter and jelly sandwich, an apple and a piece of coconut pie. Charity laughed and told him the pie would get mashed. She put in a piece of coconut cake instead with the bottle of milk. She then packed her food of a ham sandwich and a chicken sandwich, two apples, two boiled eggs, a bottle of cider and a piece of cake.

"Mamm, you promise you'll come back to me. You won't go off to be with daed and leave me, will you?" (daed - daddy)

"Jeremiah, I promise God will take care of me and of you. Don't forget to pray and learn your Bible verses. I will be back before you have time to miss me."

He jumped to hug her. "Mamm, I already miss you. I lieb you so much and don't want to lose you."

"My precious little man, you won't lose me. We will be together until we are both of a ripe old age. I promise you."

Jeremiah laughed. He grabbed his books tied with a strip of cloth and his lunch to run out and meet tante Marilyn. He would ride to school with her.

Charity ran out the back door. "Danki. Matthew or Deborah will pick him up each day."

"I know. He will be fine. Have a safe, successful trip. Rest as much as you can and take a chance to look around at different parts of the country." She chirped at the horse to start as Charity waved them goodbye. Charity went in the house wiping her eyes.

At eight fifteen Jacob pulled in to take Charity to the bus. She had said she would get her neighbor to take her in the car, but Jacob wanted to see his daughter before she left. He insisted that she take some money in case she had an emergency. He also insisted that she take her English neighbor's phone number just in case she needed to call. She laughed and hugged him, but took everything he offered.

By eight fifty they were at the bus station. There were other horse and buggies in line. Jacob got down and took her suitcase into the station for her and waited until she had purchased her ticket. He then did something that surprised her. He hugged her and kissed her cheek.

"I am so proud of you my precious dochder. You have a good business head and I know you will do well, but I must be honest and say I don't have a good feeling about this."

"Oh, daed," she laughed, "you are just worried because your chick is going where she has never been. I have never been parted from my precious zoon (son) more than a few hours, but I am going because I am trying to improve the future for him."

"Think of it as a vader (father) who loves you and wants to keep you safe and happy. Call me if you need anything."

"Daed, I lieb you, and I will be safe. I promise. Take care of Mamm and yourself and the family."

They said a final good bye and she boarded the bus. Jacob saw that her suitcase was placed in the space underneath the bus. She waved from the window as the bus pulled out. She didn't want her dad to see her anxiety, but she was naerfich (nervous). This was a big step to go to another state and travel alone.

The trip was uneventful. They stopped once at a little country convenience store to pick up passengers. They stopped next in Cleveland, Ohio.

"Folks," the big, burly bus driver announced, "we'll be stopped for about twenty minutes. There's restrooms inside and food if any of you are interested."

Charity timidly followed two older women out to use the restroom. She marveled at the mirrors and clean fixtures, but quickly took care of her business, washed her hands and grabbed her lunch bag to hurry back to the bus. She decided to eat half of a sandwich and drank some cider while they were stopped. She tried not to be bothered when people stared at her.

She had been told that it would take the bus about twelve hours to make the trip. She figured they left at nine ten that morning, so they should be in Shipshewana by nine ten in the evening. They were half way there, so she tucked her canvas bag of food under her arm and laid her head back and closed her eyes.

"Everyone off for Shipshewana" woke her up. They had arrived. She was excited and a little frightened since she had not been so far from home before.

The Like Home B & B was across the street from the bus station.

Charity timidly crossed the street and entered the home. She had not made reservations because she did not know the area. Much to her surprise and delight the B & B was owned and operated by an Amish family.

Charity introduced herself and told them she was from Shickshinny, Pennsylvania and owned and operated a store there.

She told them she was here to visit the big Yoder store.

The Amish woman came from behind the desk to take Charity's hands. "I am Erin Yoder. Welcome to Shipshewana. Do you need something to eat? It is past dinner time, but I can still get you something."

"Nee danki. I have food that I did not finish eating on the trip, but I would appreciate a hot drink."

"Please come into the kitchen. There is always coffee or tea. You can sit at the table and eat and tell me all about yourself. I am honored that you chose to stay with me."

Charity told her all about her life, her son and the death of Adam on the same night her son was born. Erin's husband, Isaiah, had come into the kitchen and sat down to talk with them. He was fascinated that Adam had taught Charity to carve items from wood.

Charity apologized and covered a yawn. "I have been up since five and did a lot of work before I left. The long trip made me very tired. Please forgive me." She finished her tea and stood.

They assured her there was nothing to forgive and asked her forgiveness for keeping her so long. Erin took her up the stairs after Isaiah had carried her bag up. It was nearly midnight.

"Will you get up on your own or do you want to be awakened at a certain time?" Erin asked.

"I have never had a real vacation. Please just let me get up when I wake up. If it is past breakfast serving, I can go to a restaurant."

"Oh, no," both Erin and Isaiah both answered. "You will be fed whenever you wish."

"Yes," Erin said. "I usually serve from six thirty to eight, but you can eat whenever you please. I want your stay to be a special one."

Erin went into a beautifully furnished room with a sleigh bed, a chest of six drawers, a low dresser with a wide mirror on it and a comfortable chair in front of it.

A hand-quilted wedding ring quilt covered the bed with matching pillow cases. A hand-hooked rug was on the floor beside the bed. She tiptoed over to open a door and was pleasantly surprised to see a bathroom. It was going to be heavenly to soak in a real tub. She turned to admire all the handmade furniture. She felt right at home.

After a good, hot bath and putting on her night clothes, she sank gratefully on a handmade feather bed. She read her Bible and had her prayers. Her eyes closed almost as soon as she got comfortable.

She woke with the sun shining through sparkling, clean windows with lovely white curtains. At first she had a jump in her heart thinking she had slept too late, then remembered where she was.

She first used the restroom and then did her Bible reading and prayer.

Charity took her time dressing carefully in her green dress with an apron over it. She carefully brushed her hair, parted it in the middle and pulled the two sides back into a neat bun at the back. Next her white prayer kapp was placed to cover the bun.

She checked herself in the mirror, giggling at herself because there were no real mirrors in her house. Satisfied with what she was seeing, she went out, carefully locked the door and put the key in her deep pocket and went downstairs.

Erin was just finishing cleaning the dining room and kitchen, but was delighted to see Charity. Isaiah was at the table reading a paper.

"Charity, guder mariye. Did you sleep well? How was the bed?"

"Guder mariye and danki. I sleep so well I almost didn't get up," she laughed. "The bed is wonderful and the feather mattress is the best. Isaiah, did you make the bed?" (guder mariye-good morning)

"Ja. Mi bruder, Emanuel, made some with me. I love to make furniture."

"Isaiah makes beautiful furniture and sells it to the English," Erin proudly answered. She then looked down because they do not believe in boasting or being proud. It was obvious she loved her husband and he loved her very much. It made Charity feel good.

"What would you like for breakfast, Charity?"

"Please, don't baddere yourself. I can go out to a restaurant."

Erin and Isaiah spoke at once. "Nee!" Isaiah grinned and then kept quiet. Erin insisted on making breakfast for Charity. "Sitz"

She hurried around and scrambled two eggs. She put these on a plate with still hot fried apples, fried potatoes, bacon and biscuits.

Charity ate and drank her coffee while they talked.

Erin refused to allow Charity to wash her dishes or clean up. Isaiah stood up. "Kumme, I will go with you to the Yoder store and introduce you to the people. My daed and two of his bruders opened the first store and now it is so big that a lot of people work there, English and Amish."

Charity was thankful that he would accompany her since she felt a little nervous about going in and asking questions. She put her black bonnet on over her prayer kapp.

They left with Erin wishing her to have a gut day. Her heart was beating erratically because she wanted to learn so

much and be able to improve and upgrade her own store.
    As it was in the next block on Van Buren, they walked.

CHAPTER THREE

Charity became ashamed of herself when she realized she was standing staring around with an open mouth. She had never seen so many items in one store and so many delightful colors. She jumped when Isaiah took her arm to introduce her to some ladies.

"This is Charity Kime from Shickshinny, Pennsylvania. She has a store there and is interested in learning about this one and what she can do to improve her store. Charity this is Rebecca Berkenstroff, Naomi Eash and Purity Yoder. These ladies are basically in charge here although there is a general manager, assistant manager and bookkeeper. They can answer your questions."

The ladies smiled and welcomed her. "We will be glad to help you any way that we can. Where would you like to start?"

"I do not know. There is so much to see and it is all so beautiful. First I would like to hear about how the store started."

Purity smiled. "I will tell you as it was my father who was one of the original owners. They first built in May, 1945 in Topeka, Indiana. The business grew and in 1952 they moved to Shipshewana. The Yoders have several stores here in a mini mall. There is a nursery with all kinds of flowers and containers next door and after that is a hardware."

"And your Bishop approves this?" Charity asked in surprise.

"He does not say anything against it because we give a good part of the profit to the work of the church for the needy."

"But you have electricity and telephones and a lot of worldly equipment."

"He knows it is necessary in a store of this size that offers so much. He also knows that those of us, who are Amish, still follow the rules and attend church. We do not act in a worldly way."

"This is so much to learn and understand."

"Now would you like to look over the store?"

"Ja danki."

They started at the end where they were. Work clothing for men of all kinds were available from coveralls to flannel shirts, jeans and Amish style clothing. Next was men's dress clothing, hats, shirts, ties for both Amish and English. The next section was clothing for women both Amish and

English. Then for children and last for babies clothing and furniture. The furniture made by Amish caused Charity to feel chocked thinking of the cradle that Adam had made Jeremiah.

She drew a deep breath of pleasure in the next department. There were tables with all kinds of covering, some Amish made and some machine made. Beautiful china, goblets and silverware were on each table. She could tell that most of the tables were Amish made.

The next section was for linens of all kinds, quilts, curtains, drapes, curtain rods, shower curtains and everything connected with bed and bath, and kitchen including pots, pans, kettles, teakettles and table grills.

Going into the next section she found all kinds of yard good, cloths, threads, yarns, needles, scissors and anything connected with sewing, knitting or crocheting. There were three quilting frames hanging from the ceiling and women around them busily quilting while laughing and talking.

The heavenly aromas told Charity where they were going next. The bakery department was manned entirely by Amish women. The display cases allowed everyone to see and drool over the products. On the shelves behind the women were cakes decorated too beautifully to cut. There were all kinds of breads and some items that Charity did not recognize. She gladly accepted their invitation to sit at a table and have some of the baked goods with a cup of coffee. She enjoyed chatting and getting to know more of the people, most of them Amish, but some of the English workers, too.

Charity was pleased to learn that they sponsored a quilting society that made quilts for babies in the hospitals or for a nursing home that the Amish had opened. She was surprised and pleased at the idea of caring for the very sick and asked if there was a home for the elderly with no relatives nearby.

"Not yet," Naomi answered, "but I imagine we will have one before long. We do take care of our own and sometimes a person does not have a relative to care for them, or the relative is too old or sick."

Charity then asked how she could get supplies to start expanding her own store. She was given name, address and phone number, as well as the person to contact for the Dunroven House and Saro Trading Company. She thanked them sincerely and prepared to leave.

Isaiah had waited patiently while talking to some of the men. He then took her to a store where she could buy pedal sewing machines and other items she would need. She purchased two sewing machines and left instructions how to send them to her.

She was very tired by now and her brain was spinning with all the good news and how she could improve her store.

Isaiah reminded her that he was hungry and it was the middle of the afternoon. She apologized to him and explained that she had been too excited to think of eating. He laughed and assured her that he knew the feeling. They walked to 'Eat A Plenty' for a light snack before they walked around more of the town and allowed Charity to see so many wondrous sights.

It finally dawned on her that she was keeping Isaiah from his house and possible work. She kept apologizing, and he kept assuring her that it was all right. By now they had walked a good distance from his home. He asked her if she wanted him to rent a horse and buggy to take them home, but she said she would prefer to walk if it was all right with him.

By the time they arrived at the house, her feet were tired and she felt she needed to change clothes. She gratefully sank into a tub of hot water and enjoyed soaking in quiet with no one banging on the door and wanting her.

It was six thirty, the time Erin had said she would serve supper. Charity hurried down to the kitchen to offer help, but was refused. Erin took her into the dining room where she met a sweet, elderly English couple celebrating sixty-five years of marriage. With a catch in her throat, Charity wished them well. She also met a thirtyish English man who was on a business trip and a young Amish couple thinking of moving to Shipshewana.

After supper, Charity insisted on clearing the table and helping that much. Later she went into the parlor to hear Erin play the pump organ. She excused herself at about nine and went up to her room to yearn for a hug from Jeremiah and to see her parents.

The next morning Charity had a quick breakfast of oatmeal, thick slices of toast with butter and jam, and coffee. She decided to walk around a little more before boarding the bus at ten to go home. She thanked Erin and Isaiah and made them promise to visit her when they got a chance.

As she walked along Van Buren, she was almost even with an alley between buildings. Three young English men, obviously drinking, came walking toward her.

"Well, will y'all lookee here. A purty little gal."

"Yeah, she's one of the prettiest I've ever seen."

"I've always wondered what they wear under those long dresses. Hey! Pull up your dress and let us see what you're wearing."

Charity, with heart fluttering wildly, turned and pretended to need to go back another way. She ignored them and hoped they would go on and leave her alone. She looked around and could only see an elderly couple on the sidewalk across the street.

One of them grabbed Charity by the left arm and swung her around.

"Now come on. You're not going high hat on us, are you?"

"Sir, I do not even know you. I am a lady minding my own business and I would appreciate you doing the same -- minding your own business."

"Hear that? She's so well mannered. She's minding her own business and she wishes I would mind mine."

They all laughed as if it were the funniest thing they'd ever heard. The elderly couple realized what was happening. The woman leaned against a store front while the man hobbled inside and told someone what was going on with the young Amish woman.

They dragged her toward the alley and all Charity could think to do was pray out loud. "Oh, Lord, I promised Jeremiah I would be safe and come back to him. I promised him he would not lose me like he did his daddy."

"Listen to that. Do you have a little boy and did you lose your husband?"

"Yes, an English man killed my husband with a car and my little boy is home with my family waiting for his mother. Please let me go. I have done nothing to you."

"Aw. We're sorry that you lost your husband. We'll make up for that."

"Please. No man has ever touched me but Adam."

"Adam. Is your name Eve?" They laughed drunkenly. "If you haven't had another man touch you we're going to give you a thrill."

Charity felt herself passing out from fright just as she was thrown to the ground on her back and hit her head on a rock. Her dress was yanked up as the man was hit with a tackle worthy of Joe Montana.

Two young men had run across from the store and knocked two of the men down. The one that had the most to drink tried to get into the scuffle, but could not control his balance. He fell on top of Charity. In a couple of seconds sirens were heard and police pulled up to take over. The three men were taken to jail and Charity was taken to Parkview Regional.

Word traveled quickly in the Amish community and Isaiah and Erin heard about it as they were eating brunch. They were angry and concerned. Erin insisted on going immediately to see about Charity. They realized how naive she was and unaccustomed to being handled so roughly.

It was late, supper time, when Charity woke to the clatter of carts and dishes. Her head hurt and she felt nauseated. She slowly turned her head when she heard her name whispered and was thankful and surprised to see

Erin and Isaiah by her bed.

"Where am I?" she croaked on a raspy throat.

"You are in Parkview Regional, a wonderful hospital, and you will get the best of care." Erin answered as Isaiah nodded and clumsily patted her hand.

"Charity, I need to call someone and tell them about this, but I do not know who to call. I know you do not have a phone where you live."

"In my case is a paper with the name of an English neighbor and their phone. Yes, my parents will want to know, but I do not want to worry them."

"I will be careful how I word the message, but I know they will want to know."

"Yes, they will. Erin, how am I? I mean what happened to me? Was I --?" She couldn't say any more. Isaiah saw she was embarrassed and tiptoed out of the room.

Erin took her hand. "No, sweet girl, you were not raped. Two English men ran just in time and knocked the drunks down. Our mayor is angry and so embarrassed that this happened to you. Your pretty blue dress was dirty and a tiny torn. I have taken it home with me to wash and repair. Did you make your dress?"

"Yes, I make all my clothes."

"I thought you might. It is very well done."

"Erin, my head feels funny."

"You hit the back of your head on a rock and have some stitches in it. You will be fine. There will not even be a scar and your hair will cover it."

"I ache all over."

"I guess you do. You are not accustomed to being thrown around and knocked down. I will leave you in peace. You will get the best of care."

"Erin! I do not have insurance and I did not bring enough money with me to pay for this."

"Do not worry, little one. Our church has a fund to cover such as this and it will. If you wish to replace it sometime in the future that will be fine." She smiled, patted Charity's leg and walked out.

With the help of an Amish nurse, Charity ate some chicken broth and jello. She drank a little lemon tea and fell asleep.

The next time she awakened it was the middle of the night and a nurse was checking on her.

"Do you need anything?"

"I would like to use the women's room, but I feel so weak."

"Don't worry, dear. I'll help you and I'll get another nurse to be sure you're fully supported." She was out of the room only a few seconds and returned with another nurse. They got her up, one on each side, and slowly walked to the restroom and helped her. When she was ready, they placed soap and hot water on a washrag and washed her hands and then rinsed them. They used another washrag to wipe her face and make her feel refreshed.

Going back to the bed she was embarrassed for a doctor to be there to see her in the hospital gown. He assured her that everyone wore them, women and men for comfort and for the doctor to work more efficiently. He shined a light in her eyes to check and then took her blood pressure and temperature.

"You have a mild concussion, so I don't want to give you a sleeping pill. Try to relax and get some rest. I'm going to have one of the nurses put an IV in your arm for nourishment and to help you relax. If you need anything or want to talk to me, just tell one of the nurses." He patted her leg under the cover and left.

She found it hard to relax thinking of Jeremiah and her family. She thanked God she was not raped and wanted to know who the men were that saved her.

The next thing she knew she was being awakened for the nurse to take stats and prepare her for breakfast. She had oatmeal, a glass of milk and apple sauce. She forced herself to eat because she knew she needed to gain strength.

She was disgusted for doing so much sleeping, but she did go to sleep.

She awakened hearing the lunch carts and dishes rattling. She smiled when the nurse asked if she minded having another breakfast. No, she would love it. She ate a scrambled egg, a bowl of grits with butter, half of a banana, and a cup of tea.

Feeling much better she noticed a huge arrangement of flowers in the room. "Are those mine?" she asked in astonishment.

"Sure are," the nurse smiled. "James Bolten and Harold Newsome sent them to you."

"Who are they and why would they send me flowers?"

"They're the two men who saved you day before yesterday."

"Has it been that long?!" she exclaimed. "I must have slept enough for several days. How can I meet the men and thank them?"

"I know them. I'll tell them you want to see them. Now rest some more."

"Rest! Rest! That is all I have done and I feel so lazy."

"Good. You'll heal much quicker then."

She didn't turn on the TV in her room because she knew that would be worldly. She could not help some of the things happening to her, but she could control her impulses. She took a drink of water and closed her eyes.

When she awakened next she was startled to hear a rustling in the room and know someone was there.

CHAPTER FOUR

Focusing her eyes, the tears rolled down her cheeks. "Mamm. You came."

"Yes, dear child and your daed and Joshua are also here. Our church prayed for you and so many wanted to come see about you, but your daed asked them to take care of your farm and the animals. We knew Matthew and Deborah were taking good care of Jeremiah and Rosemary and the girls are taking good care of the store."

At that moment the door opened and Jacob and Joshua walked in. They looked so relieved to see her awake and talking to them. They talked quietly for a short time until Joshua suggested that they leave and come back tomorrow.

"How did you get here?" Charity asked concerned.

Jenna Mae answered with a chuckle. "I think your daed would have run all the way, but we convinced him to hire a neighbor to bring us in his car. He is staying with his brother and sister-in-law until we are ready to leave."

"Where are you staying?"

"At Erin and Isaiah's bed and breakfast. Several Amish offered to take us in, but we decided to stay where you have been."

They all hugged her and left. She was lying quietly thinking and counting her blessings when the door slowly eased open. How blessed to be Amish and know everyone helped everyone else.

Her breath caught until she saw a white coat and a stethoscope around his neck.

"Oh, are you my doctor?"

"Yes, I am. My name is Dr. Isaac Yoder and I have cared for you since you came in."

She was surprised. "Are you Amish?"

"Ja. The bishop gave me permission to study if I promised to work in my own community for at least five years. I have been here four years now and looking forward to going to a smaller community."

"Why are you keeping me so long?"

"You had a mild concussion and were pretty roughed up. You would not wake up the first day. It is nature's way of protecting us from trauma. I will allow you to go with your parents tomorrow if you pass all tests. Now let me check you one more time before I leave."

She slept peacefully knowing family and friends were near. The next morning she was asked what she would like for breakfast. She had always heard of French toast, but had never eaten any. She ordered oatmeal, decaf, French toast and a slice of cantaloupe.

When the breakfast was delivered, she didn't want the syrup on the toast, but did butter the hot bread and thoroughly enjoyed it. She laughed when she was asked if she wanted anything else. "I am ashamed that I am so full now. I will look like I have been blown up like a balloon. Your food is very good and I have received excellent care."

Dr. Yoder came in and complimented her on eating a good breakfast. "It seems as if you are gaining strength. I am so happy to hear of that. Now let me run some tests and you can go with your family if everything checks out."

While she was waiting for the test results, she was surprised when two men walked into her room, smiling.

"Hello, I'm James Bolton and this is Harold Newsome. We just wanted to see for ourselves that you're all right. How do you feel?"

"Oh, you are the kind men who saved me from a horrible disaster. I can not thank you enough. If you had not heard me, I would have been in real trouble."

"An elderly couple heard you and told us. We ran over just in time. We believe that it was God's will that we be there to help you. Thank God, but you don't need to thank us. We both played football in college, so it was no trouble to run and tackle. The store owner had called the police and they were there quickly," Harold explained.

"We're just sorry, and angry, it happened in our town. Thankfully the men don't live here. They were just passing through. We've never had a problem like that before." James added.

"Thank you for the beautiful flowers. I raise flowers and sell them in my store, but no one has ever sent me any. I am grateful. Are you married and do you have children?"

"No, we're neither one married. We're going on through law school and hope to open a law practice together some day."

The door opened to allow Jenna Mae, Jacob, Joshua, Erin and Isaiah in.

There were introductions all around and much gratitude expressed to the two men who came to Charity's rescue.

James and Harold wished them God's speed and left.

They were pleased to see that Charity was better although still bruised and nursing a headache. Dr. Yoder came in and was introduced to everyone.

"Well, our girl is doing well, but still needs rest and recuperation. Keep her in bed for another day and only allow her up in small time periods. Feed her well and she will be fine in a week. I am going to release her to you and say I am so sorry to have met her under these conditions. She is a lovely young woman and a good patient." He smiled and excused himself.

In a few minutes a nurse came in offering to help Charity dress and prepare to leave. Erin gave her the dress and bloomers she had washed and mended. She had also given her a pair of her own stockings as Charity's were too torn to wear again. Isaiah had polished her shoes.

Jenna Mae had found her a prayer kapp because Charity's was lost. She had tears in her eyes because of the kindness and thoughtfulness.

A male nurse came in pushing a wheelchair which Charity declared she did not need.

"It's a rule of the hospital," he explained. "We are responsible for you until you're completely gone. I don't mean we're glad to get rid of you," he laughed.

"I understand. Bring on the contraption then. How are we getting home?"

Jacob leaned over her. "We are going in a taxi to Erin and Isaiah's B & B and stay the night. Tomorrow morning, if you feel like it, we will all go back with our English neighbor. He refused money for the trip, but we are going to see that he gets enough for gas."

"It sounds good to me. I can hardly wait to see Jeremiah."

"We did not tell him of your -- accident," Jenna Mae told her. "We knew he would be too upset and would not understand."

"Good. I promised him I would be safe and come back home to him. He was afraid I would go away like his daed."

"Well, you are going home to him and we can thank God for your safety. He provided people to help after those evil men were taken away," Joshua bristled. Charity was like his own child.

Erin served an excellent lunch of chicken and dumplings, honey-glazed carrots, deviled eggs, buttermilk biscuits, gravy, and a choice of coffee, milk or lemonade. Her dessert was pineapple upside down cake.

Charity went up to take a nap while the others talked. She began to have dreams of Adam reaching out his hand and smiling, and then of being thrown around and slung to the ground. She awakened with her mamm and Erin by her bed calling softly to her.

"Oh, dear. You frightened us with your cries. We were afraid someone had broken in and was attacking you," Erin laughed.

"You were having bad dreams," her mother explained.

"I am so sorry that I disturbed all of you. Is that daed peeping around the door?"

"It probably is. Jacob, she is all right. She was just dreaming."

Relieved he waved at them and left.

"Was I talking?"

"Only yelling no, no, no." her mother told her. "I am not surprised. You have been through a lot of disturbing things. God is with you."

"I know that, and I have the best family in the world. Wonderful, dear, sweet friends are so precious to me, also."

"Please come down and talk to us."

"Where are my shoes? I will be right down as soon as I wash my face in cold water." Jenna Mae and Erin left and went downstairs.

They talked and compared childhood stories. Some of the stories made Charity laugh when the men told of "boy tricks" they were guilty of pulling.

They had a delicious nachtesse of cornbread crumbled in a bowl with milk poured over it, pickled eggs, raw carrots and cauliflower and bread pudding with a lemon raisin sauce for dessert. (Recipes for Amish cornbread and Amish bread pudding are in my book *Amish Dilemma*. The pickled eggs recipe is on Pg. 255 in my book *A Detective's Heart*.)

"Danki, Erin. The nachtesse was wunderbaar just as you are," Jacob told her.

They all thanked her for an appeditlich nachtesse (delicious dinner). Isaiah then got the big family Biewel and read some passages. They took turn about reciting their favorite verse.

Charity humbly recited Isaiah 40:31

"Those who hope in the Lord will renew their strength. They will soar like eagles; they will run and not be weary, they will walk and not be faint." She then quoted Psalm 25, "To you, O Lord, I lift up my soul, in You I trust, O my God. Do not let me be put to shame, nor let my enemies triumph over me. God has surely been with me. He did not stop the men from hurting and scaring me, but He let me know that no evil would happen to me, and I thank Him and worship Him."

"Amen," they all responded.

"We did not know at first what was happening, but something made us pray more for you than we had been doing. Your daed and I, and I am sure the church, prayed for you from the time you left Shickshinny," Jenna Mae told her.

"Ja, I had faith that you would not do wrong, dochder," Jacob said.

"Ah, daed. I have had good home training and know what the Biewel teaches us."

They all wished each other a gut nacht and went to their own rooms for the night.

A pleasant calm settled over the town. Charity could hear faintly a violin.

CHAPTER FIVE

The next morning they were all cheerfully wishing each other a guder mariye as they sat together, with two other travelers, at the breakfast table.

Heads were bowed in silent prayer until Isaiah cleared his throat to show he was finished praying as head of the household.

The two travelers didn't say anything, but looked at each other in wonder.

They finally introduced themselves; a couple on vacation.

Erin served oatmeal with home-churned butter and fresh milk, buttermilk biscuits, scrambled eggs, bacon, melon, and coffee.

"Oh," Charity exclaimed, "Adam would have loved this. It is his favorite breakfast." She wiped her eyes and then smiled at everyone. "I can not believe I have had such a good time and am now going home with people I love. Erin and Isaiah, I can not thank you enough for your kindness and care. I appreciate it more than I can tell you."

"It is our pleasure. You have been a blessing to us," Erin declared, to which Isaiah agreed.

Jacob, Joshua and Jenna Mae thanked them over and over. They were so pleased that Charity had found such a good place to stay and with good Amish people. Jacob paid for all their rooms and the food.

Finally they were ready to leave. With tears in her eyes Charity hugged them and thanked them again. Ted Morrison was parked outside and ready to go. He had a good visit with his relatives. Jacob and Joshua again tried to give him money, but he refused.

"I wanted to make the trip. I was as worried as all of you when I heard that Charity was in the hospital. Besides, it gave me a chance to visit with relatives I haven't seen in a long time. We grew up together and were very close."

Joshua sat in the front with Ted while Jacob and Jenna Mae sat in the back with Charity between them. In spite of her ordeal, Charity was full of chatter about all she had seen and learned.

"Daed, I know what we can do to make my store more prosperous. I have ordered two sewing machines so we can make clothes at the store. I am going to add a section for fine china and items for the house. Will you add a room so that you can make furniture? You do such good work."

She talked on in her enthusiastic plans until her mother touched her knee.

She looked over and smiled fondly to see Jacob sound asleep. She reached over and held her mother's hand, happy and thankful to be with them.

They stopped in Canton, Ohio for gas, lunch and restrooms. Jacob and Joshua insisted on paying for the gas and Ted's lunch. Refreshed, they started out again. At eight they pulled into Charity's driveway. She was disappointed that Jeremiah was at Matthew's and wasn't there to greet her.

"Mr. Morrison, if I can ever do anything for you let me know. Come into my store for fresh loaves of bread and I'll be insulted if you try to pay for them. You have done so much for me and I do appreciate it."

"Charity, dear girl, I've known you all your life, and I was as worried about you as your folks were. It was a pleasure to be able to do something for you. I'll take your folks home and then get to my own home. Pearl must be anxious about me."

Charity found that Deborah had left food for her and freshly washed towels that smelled so good of the sunshine. She wasn't very hungry, but did eat a little, said her prayers, read the Biewel and went to bed.

Charity was awakened by a mass landing on her chest. Jeremiah was squealing with delight to see his mother. He could not get enough hugs and kisses.

"Mamm, my sweet mamm, you promised me you would be back. I prayed every night that you were safe and would come back to me."

"Of course I would come back to you. I could not live without my precious little man."

She breathed a prayer of thanks that no one had told Jeremiah of her horrendous experience. She knew he would not understand and would be terrified to hear of it.

"Tell me. How was school this week and did you enjoy living with oom Matthew and tante Deborah?"

"Mamm, you would not believe how wunderbaar school is. I lieb it so much and the big children let me play with them. Tante Marilyn said I am actually a second grader because you taught me so much here at home. I am adding and subtracting now and spelling big words. I can speak English."

"Darling, I hope you don't call tante Marilyn as tante in school. You must call her Mrs. Kime. The other children will not think it is fair for you to have your aunt as your teacher. They might think you get special attention."

"I do call her Mrs. in school. No, only a few of the children knew she is my tante. She explained that to me on the first day. What do we have for breakfast?" he asked excitedly jumping up and down on her.

"What would you like?"

"Pancakes!"

"All right. Let me get up, wash and dress. Goodness, look at that. It's late. It'd seven o' clock. I must be lazy this morning, and I'm so happy to be back with you."

"Don't worry mamm. Oom Mathew and oom Lawrence have already done all the work. They said to let you rest and they did the work because they lieb you."

"I will have to make them an exceptionally good nachtesse."

"YES! And I will help you. Oom Matthew took me fishing and we played ball and we went on a hike and we had a picnic and -----"

"Oh, my goodness. You had such a good time, I did not need to come back.

"Oh yes you did. I need my mamm. I lieb you so much."

"And you are so dear to me. How are the Grassdawdis?"

"All are fine."

"Good. Let us go start our day."

Charity could hardly wait to visit Leah Kime and tell her how much she appreciated Joshua and thank her for letting him come to see about her. She spent that day washing her clothes and weeding her flower garden. Vegetables were gone at this time of year. Church people had canned for her.

Soon it would be Jeremiah's seventh birthday and Charity wanted to do something special for him. He was such a good little boy and tried very hard to be the man of the house. She smiled thinking of the ways he had "helped" her.

Jenna Mae had the worst cold she had ever had. It became so hard for her to breathe that Jacob insisted she go to the hospital. They treated her and took x-rays. Dr. Alicea came to the waiting room to talk to the family. He was so serious looking that they became alarmed. Jacob stood up and demanded, "What is it?"

"Please, Mr. Startz. Sit down and I'll tell all of you." They sat expectantly and he took a deep breath. "Mrs. Startz has cancer of the lungs and it has spread too far for us to treat it successfully. She can take chemo and live another three or four months, but, truthfully, it would be awfully hard on her."

"Da Herr sei mit du." Jacob spoke so low Dr. Alicea strained to hear.

"What did he say?" he asked looking at Charity. Matthew and Lawrence sat on either side of their daed. Alicia, Maeve and Joseph sat as close to Charity as they could get. Charity was glad Jeremiah was at home with the pregnant Deborah.

Charity looked sorrowfully at Dr. Alicea. "He said the Lord is with us."

"It is Gottes wille," Jacob whispered and turned to accept the hug from Joshua and Leah who had come to join them.

"Did he just say it is God's will?" Dr. Alicea asked.

"Ja," Matthew answered. "We leave everything in God's hands."

"Does that mean she won't be taking chemo or other treatments?"

"How much life can you promise her and will it be free of pain?" Jacob asked with a catch in his throat.

"I can't promise anything. You're right. It's up to God. I can only say, from past experience the patient has from six months to a year. It's often less. And sometimes there is pain."

"Then we can take her home?" Matthew asked in a trembling voice.

"You can or you can leave her here where we can make her comfortable and ease her pain." Dr. Alicea was trying to be honest with them.

"Could we leave her with you for a while to ease her pain and then take her home? She will want to go to meet her Lord in her own bed," Jacob asked sadly.

"We can do that and if you want, and we can send a home health nurse with her to use some of the same medicine we will use. The law prevents me from giving it to you to use."

"Let us talk about it as a family including Jenna Mae and I will give you an answer very soon." Jacob was fighting sobs by now.

"That's fine with me. I'll be praying for you and God bless you all."

The entire Startz family gathered in Charity's home. They were joined by the Kime family as they were considered family. Belinda and Mary Sue were the only children left after Adam was killed.

First they had Biewel reading and then prayer. There was heartache, but strong belief in God and in a place in Heaven for each of them.

"Let not your hearts be troubled. You believe in God, believe also in Me. I in my Father's house am many mansions. I am going there to prepare a place for you." (Part of John 14:1-3) *"Because I live, you also will live."* (John 14: 19) Also Revelation 21:4 *(in Heaven)* *"He will wipe away every tear from their eyes. There will be no more death or mourning or crying or pain."*

After Joshua prayed, they sadly looked at each other not knowing how to start the conversation. Jacob cleared his throat of the lump there. "We all love her and selfishly do not want to give her up. She is going to be in a lot of pain; she has been in pain and would not complain. All of you know what the doctor has said. How will we tell Jenna Mae?"

"The truth," Charity spoke through her tears. "Mamm can handle the truth and she would want to know. She loves her Lord and will not fear dying, but she will hate to leave all of us."

"She is only forty-eight," Leah said with sadness.

"Do we have to tell her so soon?" Lawrence asked.

"As Charity said, she will want to know," Matthew spoke.

Alicia, Maeve and Joseph, Belinda and Mary sat still and sorrowfully. All of them were old enough to understand except Jeremiah.

"How can I tell Jeremiah?" Charity sobbed. "He loves all of you so much."

"Hold off telling him until near the end. He will need to know she is very sick, but he does not need to be told she is dying." Jacob spoke solemnly.

"We can then tell him then that she is going to be with his daed in Heaven."

"So what are we going to do now?" Lawrence asked.

Joshua cleared his throat. "May I speak?"

"Of course," they chorused.

"Jenna Mae knows she is sick. She does not need to know how little time she has. Why not love her and make her as comfortable as possible. Ask the Bishop and the Ministers to come pray with her. That will be a natural thing they do. Everyone needs to keep a cheerful face around her and try to make her feel she is wanted and needed."

There was a long silence. Leah and Joshua looked at each other. "Ja," Jacob said, "we can do that. It makes sense. I just hope the doctor does not tell her until we talk to him."

Charity and Alicia served cake and hot cider to everyone. Jeremiah was already in bed. The Kimes then left to go home. Matthew and Lawrence followed. Alicia, Maeve and Joseph waited on their daed. They all hugged Charity and quietly left.

Charity lay in bed trying not to cry. *I do not want Jeremiah to hear, besides it would serve no purpose. I will ask Rosemary and the Zook twins to help more in the store so that I will be free to help with mamm.*

CHAPTER SIX

Sheriff Micah Fleming had volunteered to drive Jacob's family to the hospital. He was there by eight the morning following the family get-together to discuss Jenna Mae.

"I'm not going to ask you how your are," Micah said. "Anita wants me to bring you to the house for breakfast. We can't go into the hospital until visiting hours at ten."

"Thank you, but we ate early," Jacob answered.

"I know you did, but you've never tasted Anita's home-made cinnamon rolls. We can have a cup of coffee and a roll while we catch up on what all has been going on. We heard Jenna Mae is sick, but we don't know any of the particulars. She always seems so strong and healthy. We're very worried."

Micah and Anita had twin boys who were now five years old. They also had a three year old, Elizabeth Ann, who had her daddy wrapped around her little finger. They had tried for six years to have a child and everyone had prayed with them. The children were a delight of their hearts, but they kept Anita close home.

"We would love to come with you," Charity spoke for them which earned her a glare from Jacob. "Let me get Jeremiah going for Lawrence to take to school and I will be ready. Charity was always outspoken for an Amish woman.

Matthew and Jacob shifted from foot to foot not knowing what to say. Seventeen year old Alicia, sixteen year old Maeve and fifteen year old Joseph were staying at home to help Lawrence.

Alicia was eagerly looking forward to rumspringa. This is a period of time, usually a year, in which Amish youth are permitted to be worldly. If they have not been baptized, the church has no control over them. They can move to the city or nearest town with friends to experience all that the auslanders (outsiders) do.

At the end of the time, or before, the youth decides whether to join the church and be Amish or stay outside and give up their family and Amish friends. If they decide to stay outside, they can no longer come home to live. They can visit, but the community, as a whole, will ignore them. A few do make the decision to stay outside and work and live, but the majority remains Amish and come home to be baptized.

Before they are baptized and join the church, they are in a training class for several weeks to learn Bible verses and the history of their religion. On the day of baptism the whole church congregates. The Bishop asks the congregation if they are willing to accept these young people and promise to help them in their faith. Of course they always answer yes.

They feel that the young people belong to everyone. If a young person is observed acting badly or doing wrong, any adult nearby will speak sternly to them.

The girl's white prayer kapp is removed leaving her head bare for the last time in public. The boys have removed their hats upon entering the building.

The Deacon steps forward holding a wooden bucket of water and a tin cup. The youths kneel and the Bishop cups his hands to receive water. He goes to each one saying, "I baptize you in the name of the Father (places Amish Promise water on the head), the Son (water) and the Holy Ghost (water). He then asks them to stand and says, "Upon your faith which you have confessed before God, and these many witnesses. You are baptized in the name of the Lord, and of the church, we extend to you the hand of fellowship. Rise and be a faithful member of the church." The Bishop then gives the boys a Holy Kiss on the cheek and the Deacon's wife gives the girls the kiss. There is rejoicing and a big feast follows.

Amish youth are not permitted to have a courtship or a "steady" until they are sixteen. There is no kissing or being together where no one can see them. A boy obtains a courting buggy which is open so everyone can see who is in it and what they are doing.

Charity was concerned about Alicia because she was basically shy and had not had any experience with meeting auslanders.

Lawrence came to pick up Jeremiah and speak to his daed. "Tell mamm I lieb her and my heart is with her."

"Ja. I will, son. Have a good day, but try to get as much work done as you can."

By eight thirty-five Jacob got in the front seat with Micah while Charity and Matthew got in the back. They were quiet on the way to the Fleming house.

Anita was delighted to see them and hugged each one. She knew the Amish men were not hugged as a general rule, but she honestly cared about this family.

The children were well-mannered and went to a play room that Micah had built for them on the back of the house. The boys had a fort made from an old refrigerator box laying on its side. In it were tin soldiers and other items that interested them. Elizabeth Ann went to a hobby horse and rode to her heart's content. She then took dolls to a big doll house and served them teas on a tiny set of dishes.

They always played well together. Sometimes the boys would play a board game with their little sister. Their daddy had taught them they must be manly and protect her and be kind. It was only natural that there would be disagreements, but not often.

The Startz family could hardly wait to visit Jenna Mae in the hospital. Charity could never remember her mother being sick enough to be in bed for more than a couple of days and certainly never in the hospital. Jacob's heart was heavy. This was the woman he loved and married and still loved her as much as he did the day he married he. He was sure she felt the same about him. Theirs had been an ideal marriage, working together, loving together and sharing all their life's happenings. He did not want to think of having to go on living without her, but if God wanted her with Him, then what could anyone here on earth do.

Micah and Anita shed tears when they heard that Jenna Mae was dying. They loved her, too. They tried to comfort the Startz family and insisted on them having coffee and rolls. Soon it was time to go.

They thanked Anita for a lovely visit and expressed their appreciation for the ride. The Flemings were honestly glad to have them and to be able to help.

Jenna Mae looked so rested, and was smiling so brightly, that it was difficult to believe she would not be with them much longer. She was glad to see them and ready to come home.

"What did the doctor say is wrong with me? Can I go home today?" She was anxious. The family didn't know what to say.

Matthew finally spoke. "Mamm, we are going now to talk to the doctor and ask him to tell us everything. We will come right back and tell you."

They hurriedly left her room and went to keep the appointment with Dr. Alicea.

A nurse brought in additional chairs for them in the doctor's office. Dr. Alicea looked kindly at them. "Well, what have you decided?"

Jacob cleared his throat. He couldn't seem to talk. "How long will it be before she is in a lot of pain?"

"That varies according to the individual. Jenna Mae is in an advanced stage, so I would say she will be in a lot of pain. Six months may be a real guess. She is still cheerful and cooperative though."

"Have you, or a nurse, given her any idea that she is dying?" Matthew asked.

"No. I gave specific orders that her condition was not to be discussed. If she had been coming in for regular yearly check-ups, it's possible this could have been caught a long time ago, but it has been years since she had a check-up."

"Dr. Alicea. Would you be willing to explain this to her? My mother is strong in her Lord and will be able to listen and accept it," Charity asked.

"That's one of the sad duties of a physician. It is especially sad for me since I know and admire all of you so much. Yes, I can tell her and you can be present if you wish."

"We wish," Jacob declared.

Jenna Mae's room was crowded with everyone standing around. She greeted them with a big smile which quickly faded when she saw the solemn expressions on their faces. "Tell me," she said softly.

Dr. Alicea took her hand and patted it. "Dear lady, it breaks my heart to tell you, but you have cancer of the lungs. We can treat it, but it would have been a different story if you had been coming in for regular check-ups. We just have to be more aggressive now."

"I am dying," she said. "I am ready to claim my mansion with my Lord."

By now the family was crying. Matthew stepped to the bed and took her hand. He leaned over and kissed her cheek. "Mamm, we are all dying. Remember you told me once that once we are born, every day we live is one closer to dying. Just take the care that Dr. Alicea wants to give you and we will all help.

Jenna Mae looked around the room. "Charity, I have been saving something for Jeremiah for his birthday. It is in my hope chest. You will see what it is when you look."

Charity was trying so hard to be in control of her emotions. "Mamm, it is only three weeks until Jeremiah's birthday. You will be there to give it to him. He will love whatever you give him, especially if it is something you have made."

"Sure mamm," Matthew chocked, "you will be there and be the life of the party."

"What party?" Charity demanded. "I did not plan a party."

Matthew scowled at her. "Yes, you will have a party." He stared so hard at her that she realized he was sending her a message.

"I guess you are right. A party would please Jeremiah."

'Well, that's settled," Dr. Alicea laughed. "Let's all go out now and let this lady rest. If she is doing well tomorrow morning, she can go home with you. I will send a nurse to make sure she is getting her medications and rest."

Micah met them in the lobby. "How is she? I didn't try to come up because there's enough of you. I didn't want to tire her."

"She knows she is dying, but she does not know how soon," Jacob gulped and wiped his eyes. "She is a woman so full of courage and love of her Lord and her family. We will make her comfortable and try to be happy around her. We can not tell Jeremiah so soon. He might let it slip and he would not understand."

"Will she have the chemo treatments?" Micah asked.

"Nee. No. There is no hope in such treatments."

"I see. Do you need to go anywhere else before you go home?"

"Thank you, no. We just need to get home and make a bed for mamm in the front room where she can see everything and all that is going on," Matthew told him.

"Will you need help moving furniture? I'll be happy to help."

"No, thank you. Lawrence and I can do most of it."

"Okay. Get in then and let's get you home."

But mamm, you have not told me why Grossmudder Startz must stay in bed so much. Is she sick?"

"Yes, my little man. Grossmudder is very sick and we must be cheerful around her and make her feel better." Charity tried not to cry.

"What is wrong with her, mamm?" Jeremiah asked worriedly.

"She has a very bad cold in her lungs and has trouble breathing. We are going to keep her warm, comfortable and happy."

"I can do that," he said, strutting around.

"Of course you can. You are my little man."

"Mamm, what am I getting for my birthday?"

"Who said you were getting anything? You know as Amish we do not party much."

"I know, but I heard you tell oom Lawrence that oom Matthew wanted to have a party for my birthday."

"Oh, sometimes big ears hear sad things. How do you know we were talking about you?"

"Because he said it would be good for Grossmudder and give her something to think about."

"Well, why not wait and see what happens. Surprises are much nicer than when you know something is going to happen. If you did have a party, is there someone at school you would like to have at your party?"

"Oh, yes!" He proceeded to name everyone except one boy.

"Why did you not say Benjamin Hersberger's name?"

"He is so mean and no one likes him."

"Maybe he is not mean at all. Maybe he just needs to know he has a friend."

"Do you think that would keep him from being mean if I invited him to my party?"

"Well, it might, if you were going to have a party. Now why are you still up? Go take a bath and get ready for bed."

He scurried away happily thinking of his birthday which would be soon.

The weeks did fly by. Jenna Mae was taken care of with a lot of love. Jacob had dared any of them to act as if she were on her deathbed. He said, "Do as much of the work as you can, but don't make a big deal out of it. Keep her from lifting or getting over tired."

Jenna Mae seemed to be getting some strength back. She was so pleased to be asked to give suggestions for the party for Jeremiah.

"Charity, I will give Jeremiah something very special on his birthday. I will tell you on that day to get it for me."

"Danki, my sweet mamm. I lieb you so much. You do not need to get anything for him. He knows you lieb him and he adores you."

"I know, but this is special and I have been saving it for him. I would have given it to him before now because I may be with his daed in Heaven soon and I want him to have it."

"Oh, mamm. You will be here to guide us and lieb us for a long time."

Musical instruments were frowned upon as being of the world, but harmonicas could be played. Charity asked two of the boys to play for games for the party as some English were also invited. They were very pleased to be of service. They practiced together many times and had a group following them to enjoy the music and singing.

The big day finally came and Jeremiah could hardly contain himself. He got up at five thirty and ran out to do his chores. He then ran over to Grossdawi Startz to see if he had any work for him to do and, of course, to remind them that today he is seven and big enough to do a lot of work.

Oom Lawrence felt of the muscles in his arms and was properly impressed with the size of them. Jeremiah strutted back to the house so pleased with himself that he forgot to be humble and not proud. He was barefoot and so caught up with the idea of his party and maybe presents that he did not notice the snake coiled among the tobacco plants as he ran along.

It had been cold so the snake fortunately was sluggish and made a half-hearted attempt to uncoil to strike. The movement was seen by Jeremiah and he yelled jumping straight up and taking off running yelling, "Snake, snake."

Oom Matthew happened to hear him and laughed saying, "There are no snakes around. It is too cold for them. They have all gone into a hole for the winter." He was shocked to see the big fat copperhead in the tobacco field. "He must have been greedy and decided to eat a little longer and it got too cold for him," he said as he chopped the snake to pieces. "There. He will not be around to bite anyone."

Jeremiah realized that he could not go without his shoes until next summer. As he thought about it, yes, it was cold, but he had been so eager to talk about his party, he had run out of the house without shoes.

Charity was so frightened when he told her about the snake. She wondered what it was doing on their property when the horses and mules hooves hitting the ground usually scared the snakes away. It was nothing to think about now.

Alicia and Maeve came to help her prepare for the party. The day before they had baked six dozen cupcakes and a big birthday cake, a banana split cake which was Jeremiah's favorite. There was also fruit slush for the younger ones.

Deborah waddled in complaining about not being able to see her feet and how big and fat she was. She had made some new clothes for Jeremiah. Matthew had bought him a bat with a small ball attached to it. Jeremiah would enjoy trying to keep the ball bouncing by hitting it with the bat.

Lawrence had gotten a checker board and checkers for him. Jacob and Joshua together were going to give him his own horse. That was a big surprise.

Charity had bought new shoes instead of having the cobbler make them. She had also made him a new suit just like his ooms. She was so filled with love for him and everyone, but she had never forgotten Adam.

Eighteen children and forty-three adults showed up for Jeremiah's party. He was strutting all over the place so pleased with himself. Several of the adults cautioned him about being too proud, but he just grinned at them and went on with his form of happiness.

The game "The Road To Jerusalem" was a big hit with the children and the adults cheered and laughed with it. Nine chairs were sat facing one direction. Eight more chairs were behind them facing the other direction. The children began marching around the chairs while Oliver Snader and Buckley Yoder played their harmonicas. Without warning the boys would stop playing. The children struggled to get seated. The one left out had to leave the game. That child was given a cupcake. A chair was removed making one less chair than children marching. This went on until only one child was left. Jeremiah was disappointed that he was not the winner, but he smiled and congratulated Mordecai Hershberger as he gave Mordecai a checker game in a box. All the little boys loved marbles. Charity knew the marbles would not be left in that box for long. They would be out on the ground in a marbles match.

"Drop The Handkerchief" was the next game. The children stood in a circle. Jeremiah started walking around the outside. He dropped the handkerchief behind one of the girls thinking she would be too slow to catch him. If he had gotten away, she would be the one walking around. As it was, when he dropped the cloth, he took off running, but Amelia Klopfenstein had grown up with a bunch of brothers and she had learned to run fast. She ran and tagged him, so Jeremiah had to keep walking and try to choose someone else so he could run back to his spot without being tagged. The person who didn't catch him would then go around and try to find someone to chase them.

After ten minutes, Charity called a halt to this game. The Amish, as a rule, did not play games, but special permission had been given for this party. All of the children were out of breath and excited. They had to sit at a table and wait for a blessing to be asked, then they could eat.

They enjoyed the Banana Split cake and the Fruit Slush to drink. There was also homemade ice cream made with fresh strawberries. After they had eaten, Jeremiah opened his gifts and politely thanked each one for them.

Jeremiah whirled around to see why the children were wide-eyed and oohing. Jacob and Joshua walked to him leading a beautiful coal black Friesian yearling. The little gelding was high stepping and feeling frisky this cool September morning.

"Jeremiah," Grossvader Jacob said, "this baby is too young to be ridden, but by the time we help you get him trained, you will be ready to ride and have a great horse."

Charity had no idea they were going to give him a horse, and she was very concerned. "Oh, he looks like a handful. Jeremiah, promise me you will never get near this horse unless an adult is with you. He is young and does not understand any more than little boys understand about danger."

"Is he really mine?" Jeremiah asked breathlessly with round eyes. "I can really have him and train him?"

"Yes," answered Grossvader Joshua, "but only if one of us is with you.

In his excitement Jeremiah forgot English and lapsed into Amish. "Oh, grandfathers, I love him all ready and I will promise to wait for an adult to be with me. May I name him?"

"Jeremiah!" Charity scolded. "You are forgetting something."

He looked puzzled and then, with a big grin, turned to hug both grandparents and say a sincere, "Danki."

Grossmudder Jenna Mae was rapidly getting too tired to stay up much longer. She had waited many months to give Jeremiah her gift. "Jeremiah, come here to me. I have something very special for you. Do you remember all the pictures I painted that you liked so much, the ones of the horses plowing and the field of wild flowers?"

"Ja, Grossmudder. I remember. They are beautiful."

"You know we do not have our picture taken because it would be making a graven image."

"Ja, I know."

"I have painted something very special for you." She handed him two pictures about twelve by fourteen that she had painted. One was of a man with a beautiful chestnut horse and one was of just the man's smiling face.

"Who is this?" he asked as Charity looked over his shoulder and gasped.

"It is your daed, Jeremiah. He is with Bonnie Kate and he is smiling at you because he is so proud that you have grown to be a good young man." She wiped her eyes and went to hug her mother.

"Danki, mamm. Now he can know what his daed looked like. In fact Jeremiah is beginning to look just like him."

Leah looked at them and wiped her eyes. "Ja, it is my precious boy."

"Danki all of my loved ones. You have made me so happy. Danki all my friends for your gifts. Danki for coming."

"Gern gshehn" was called out many times. (You are welcome)

Jeremiah threw his arms around Charity's neck and hugged her until she laughingly begged for mercy. "It has been a wunderbaar day."

The adults, and a few of the children, stayed to share a nachtesse of chicken, ham, deviled eggs, coleslaw, green beans, squash, biscuits and gravy, cake, ice cream and fruit slush as well as buttermilk, coffee or cider.

There were many fond gut nachts and everyone went home. A tired, but excited, happy boy listened to the reading of the Biewel, said his prayers and was fast asleep.

CHAPTER SEVEN

Jeremiah was up early to do his chores and visit with his new horse. He wanted to think of a very good name. He ran out to the barn, but even though it was five thirty, Jacob and Matthew were already there doing the work.

"Guder mariye," Jeremiah yelled happily while jumping around. "Where's my horse?"

"He is in my barn," Matthew answered, "and you must not be so excited around him. He is very young remember and will be easily frightened."

"Have you thought of a name?" Jacob asked him.

"No," he answered slowly, "but I'm still thinking. It must be something very special."

While the men finished feeding the animals and milking the cow, Jeremiah ran to gather the eggs and check to see that the hogs were fed. He ran into the house with a basket full of fresh eggs.

"Mamm," he yelled, "can we have scrambled eggs and pancakes?"

"Oh, my darling little man, when are you going to learn how to talk without yelling? I can hear you very well."

"I am just so happy that I can not help it."

She hugged him and as usual spoke a prayer of thanks for him and thinking that she still loved Adam.

"Mamm, will you get married? Tobias Hershberger's wife died and he then married Marcella Lepman."

"Tobias had four small children that needed a mother. You and I are doing just fine together. And I have my daed and bruders to help as well as two sisters. I loved your daed so much that no other man could take his place in my heart."

"You also have Grossmuder Startz, and all the Kime family."

"Yes, I know, and I am so thankful to have the blessing of loved ones. Now we must eat and get ready for church. We meet at the Klopfensteins today. Matthew and Deborah will pick us up at seven forty-five."

Before church everyone was asking about Jenna Mae and saying they were praying for her. Maeve and Alicia had stayed at home with her. She would not admit it, but she was getting weaker. All of the rest knew the time was near to release her to claim her mansion with the Lord as she worded it.

At eight the service began and would continue until eleven. Isaac Slabough led the singing. Pastors Amos Snader and Joseph Lehman had prepared their sermons and were anxious to get started. Deacon Moses Verkler, now very old and frail, stood to give a few announcements and to ask for help for a church member.

Moses Yoder had been the Bishop for some time and was getting too old to carry the burden. They knew they would need to vote on a new Bishop soon. Moses just sat and smiled because he was going deaf.

When the time would come to select a new Bishop, the church members were asked to write a name on a slip of paper that they recommended. The present Bishop, Deacon and Pastors selected four of the names that were given most often. A Bible verse, Acts 1:21-26, was written on a slip of paper. The disciples voted and selected a man to replace

Judas, therefore, the Amish were going to select another man to replace the Bishop. The Bible verse would be placed in a hymn book. Three other empty books would be placed beside it. No one knew which book held the verse. The four men selected would step forward and pick up a hymnal. The one holding the Bible verse would be the new Bishop by God's choice.

After the service the ladies hurried to prepare the food and the men gathered outside to talk, even though it was cold. October was never a warm month. The talk was of the election coming in the United States, for President and other officers, and how it would affect their taxes.

After a delicious, filling meal of ham, meat loaf, chicken, pickled beets, squash, green beans, potatoes, strawberry rhubarb pie with coconut cake and almond joy cake. Beverages were as usual, coffee, tea, milk, water.

Charity helped clean while the men put the benches back on the hauling wagon. Deborah complained of a stomach ache and sat down a lot. No one minded, but Charity kept a worried eye on her.

On the way home, Deborah cried out with a pain in her lower back and in her stomach. Matthew did not want to run the horse, but hurried as fast as he thought safe. He was extra careful watching for English cars.

They arrived at the Startz home and Lawrence ran to help unhitch the horse and rub her down. Just as Matthew was almost carrying Deborah and helping her in the house, her water broke on the front porch. She was so embarrassed, but Charity assured her it was natural. Jeremiah was bug-eyed at the happenings. He had never experienced such a thing.

Matthew was going around in a whirl of decisions. Should he risk rushing Deborah to the hospital or should he call for a midwife? The baby was early.

Would there be time for the hospital? Charity took charge and ran to a neighbor to take Deborah in their car to the hospital. Lawrence would stay at home with Jeremiah, his mother and the girls. Jeremiah was full of questions and very frustrated because no one had time or care to sit and explain things to him. He decided he would just go outside and go away.

What Matthew and Charity did not yet know was that when Deborah gave birth to a beautiful eight pound six ounce girl, Jenna Mae went to meet her Creator and Jeremiah had wandered off and was lost.

Maeve ran to tell the Bishop, crying all the way. She stopped to tell a couple of women who would come help prepare the body. The women would wash the body and the hair. They would place a white dress on her or the one in which she was married. A white prayer kapp would be placed on the bun on the back of her head. No cosmetics or jewelry. There is no embalming.

The men would make a plain pine box (coffin) for her with nothing on it and no lining. The front room, where she had her bed, would be cleared of all furniture except for a table for the coffin to lie on. It was standard practice to have a wake and a funeral within three days.

People would come bringing food. This would be the first of three viewings. On the second day again food would be brought and there would be a service. The Pastors would read Bible verses followed by silent prayer. The Bishop would give a short sermon on their belief in eternity and the after life.

The name of the deceased would not be spoken and there was no eulogy or singing. People would file past to look at the body. Parents would sometimes lift children so they could see.

The coffin is closed and placed on a special black wagon pulled by black horses. The black buggies sometimes line up for a mile. Police help with the traffic. If the Amish Cemetery is a distance, special permission is given to use a black English hearse. Grave markers are wooden with nothing written on them. Wood is used because it will rot in time showing that life is not long. The church keeps a directory of the place of graves in case someone wants to visit there in the future. The family rarely goes back because they believe that everything is in God's hands.

At the grave service there is no singing and there has been no music all these days. Bible verses are quoted; sometimes the words of a song are read. The coffin is opened for one last viewing. Men place ropes around the coffin and place it in a bigger wooden box. There are no flowers or any other worldly items. Just dirt over the plain grave. The men fill in the grave. The women have again brought food and all go back to the home of the deceased to eat together

Deborah was kept in the hospital for a couple of days. When the neighbor brought Matthew and Charity home about five o'clock, they were shocked to hear Jenna Mae had died while they were gone. When Charity hunted for Jeremiah, and no one had seen him for almost three hours, she was beside herself. She forgot everything but finding her precious son.

The women had come to help wash the body and dress it for viewing searched. The men rode out in all directions to find Jeremiah. Charity was torn between fright at what might happen to him and anger that he would put them all through this.

It began to get dark and cold. Everyone was very concerned for fear he had been abducted or hit by a car and was lying in a ditch. They checked the river behind Charity's house, but no little boy.

Anthony Zook didn't help when he remarked, "Thank God it is too cold for poisonous snakes to be out, but there is a gang of rogue dogs running around stealing chickens and once was after my little pigs. They could tear a small boy apart."

Fortunately Charity didn't hear him or she would have been crazy with worry. She was in a buggy with Nadine and Benjamin Lapp calling out for Jeremiah as they drove up one country road after another.

Everyone gathered back at the Startz home for hot chocolate, biscuit, egg and bacon sandwich and to warm up and rest. Some of the men were still out on horseback hunting off the road.

Buckley Yoder, riding his favorite horse, a chestnut Arabian stallion named Chief Warrior, found Jeremiah lying in the Snader corn field fast asleep. He had twisted his ankle and cried himself to sleep. Buckley carefully lifted him on the horse in front of him and hurried to the Startz home.

Charity was so relieved to see her son that she fainted for the first time in her life.

Matthew, Lawrence, Jacob and Joshua sat Jeremiah down and gave him a good talking. They knew Charity would not approve because she did nothing but scold him a little. The men thought he needed a good spanking, but they waited for Charity to stir. Jeremiah was properly disciplined because he had not known such a scolding before. He was embarrassed and half way frightened. His heart was heavy because his loved ones were not happy with him. And his ankle hurt.

They all waited until Charity could be with him to tell him of his Grossmudder Startz death.

Charity came into the room, wild-eyed with grief. "Oh, Jeremiah. How could you do this to us? I was so worried; everyone was worried. People have been out looking for you when they needed to be home milking cows, feeding animals and taking care of their children. Please tell me why you disappeared and caused so much trouble for everyone."

By this time Jeremiah was sobbing. "I am so sorry, mamm. I did not mean to cause trouble, but no one was paying attention to me and would not talk to me and explain what was going on. Grossmudder Startz is so sick, then tante Deborah peed all over the porch and everyone got excited and rushed around. You left with oom Matthew and did not say a word to me."

Joshua took Jeremiah on his lap. "Jeremiah, tante Deborah did not pee on the porch. The water that was in the sack carrying the baby broke and the baby was ready to be born."

"But she went to the hospital to find a baby."

"Oh, dear," Charity wailed, "I must have failed in my teaching. Come to think of it, I have never discussed this with him."

"For goodness sakes," barked Lawrence, "the boy lives on a farm. Surely he has seen the birth of an animal."

"I think not. I have always been careful to shield him from it."

"What about an animal being born?" Jeremiah asked puzzled.

Noah Kime, Joshua's brother, happened to be in the room. "I have a cow that will be giving a late birth in a few days. He is welcome to watch that."

"Yes! Oh, yes. May I mamm?"

"I do not think so. You are too young."

Joseph Startz laughed loudly. "I was younger than Jeremiah when I saw the birth of a horse and a cow. He is not too young."

Jacob turned quickly on Joseph. "Have you forgotten so soon that we have a grief here?"

"No. Sorry daed."

"What grief is he talking about mamm?"

Charity took a deep breath and hugged Jeremiah on her lap. "Grossmudder Startz went to Heaven tonight to live with your daed."

"When will she be back?"

"There is no coming back. They live in Heaven and wait on us to get old and join them."

"Will I go to Heaven and see them when I get old?"

"Yes, my little man, you probably will -- when you get old."

"Will you go with me mamm?"

"Oh, Jeremiah, I will probably be there before you because I am older than you are."

"But Mamm, you have got to wait on me," he said excitedly.

"Do not worry about it now. That will come many years from now. Get down now and we need to go home. I will return early tomorrow morning Daed. Or do you need me for something now?"

"I love you, daughter, but Alicia, Maeve and Joseph are here. I think Lawrence is staying, also."

"All right. Jeremiah, why are you limping?"

"I jumped over the ditch to get into the Snader's corn field and hurt my ankle." He began to limp more realizing that she was concerned and he could get more attention.

Lawrence offered to give him a piggy-back ride home, which he gladly accepted. Charity's heart was filled with grief and could not laugh with them, but she was relieved that Jeremiah was home safe. She loved her mother and would miss her, but she was glad her mother was not suffering. They believed in Revelations 21:4 "There will be no more tears, sorrow, suffering, pain or grief."

Charity started to give Jeremiah his usual bath, but he stopped her.

"Mamm, I am big enough now to give myself a bath. I will do a good job, too."

Charity was shocked and a little hurt. Her baby was growing up and she wanted him to stay little for a longer time. She knew this was impossible.

"Yes, my little man. I know you will do a good job; behind your ears and around your neck as well as your toes." She tickled him and had him laughing as he went to take his bath.

He came down with his hair still damp wearing his nightshirt, a house coat and bedroom slippers. Charity was pleased that he had remembered to wash his hair.

"Mamm, can I read from the Biewel tonight? You said I am the man of the house."

"May I," she corrected him. "Of course you may," she said, reaching to draw him on her lap.

"No, mamm, I am too big to be sitting on your lap now," he said with a great deal of importance.

Her heart sunk. Already she was losing her baby. With tears in her eyes she asked him what he was going to read.

"Well, I like a lot of verses, but I think I will read Psalm 23."

"That is an excellent selection."

He read with a lot of importance because he loved to read and he was a good reader. He finished and they had prayer.

"Mamm, do you think we can talk about my daed and Grossmudder?"

"What would you like to talk about?"

"Can we just remember? I would like to hear about daed while I am holding his picture that Grossmudder painted for me. Then tell me stories about when you were little with Grossmudder."

Charity chocked back the tears and talked with him for over half an hour.

"You little minx. You have talked past your bed time. Get up to bed."

"Mamm, I think I have finally thought of a name for my horse."

"Marvelous. What did you decided upon?"

"I would like to name him Adam J. That way it would be about both my daed and my Grossmudder."

"I think that would be a splendid name." She tucked him into bed and pulled the covers up. When she stooped to kiss his cheek, he protested that he was too old for that.

"I know you love me and I love you, but we can love each other without hugging and kissing. But I see oom Matthew and tante Deborah kissing. Oh, I forgot. What did they name the baby? Was it a boy?"

"They have not decided for sure, but I think they will name her Jenna Louise after both Grossmudders. Matthew's mother Jenna and Deborah's mother, Louise."

"What will she be to me?"

"She will be your cousin and you will be big enough to help take care of her and teach her all good things."

"That is very nice," he yawned, "but why didn't they get a boy? He would have been more fun." He was asleep before Charity could leave the room.

CHAPTER EIGHT

The service and burial of Jenna Mae was attended more than others had been. English and Amish participated because everyone knew her and loved her. Too, the English had a great deal of respect for Charity. They knew her and liked her through her business at the store. More than two hundred people came to the house to eat together.

The weeks flew by and Thanksgiving was the next Thursday. Charity was feeling very sad because she remembered what delicious, huge meals her mother always cooked and had an open door policy for anyone who wished to eat with them.

She talked to Matthew and Lawrence about the dinner. They agreed that everyone would come to Charity's for dinner as it would be too sad for her daed to have it at his house. Alicia, Maeve, Deborah and Mariah Slabough who was the girl Lawrence was preparing to marry, would help. Everyone would furnish some of the food and the majority of it would be cooked at Charity's.

The Kime family and the Slaboughs would come by later for dessert and beverage. Charity asked Matthew and Lawrence to carry in the big picnic table for the back yard and set it in a corner for the children. She rolled back the wall between the kitchen and the sitting room and placed a longer table beside the kitchen table.

She did not care if people frowned at her. She was going to break tradition and have everyone eat together instead of the men eating first and then the women. Matthew,

Lawrence and Joseph did not care, but they knew their daed, being old traditionalist, would be upset. They all knew how much he loved Charity though and thought she would be able to carry it off.

Charity had ironed lace table cloths to place over the plain white cloths. She also ironed the white cloth napkins. China and glasses were polished until everything was shining. She tied a big apron around Jeremiah and let him polish the tableware. He felt very big and important.

She had washed windows, polished furniture and mopped floors until she was so worn out she was afraid she might not be able to do much for the dinner. The night before the dinner she made eight dozen yeast rolls, one hundred cookies, a big bowl of potato salad and Jeremiah's favorite Banana Split cake. She was up early and did the outside chores, then hurried in, washed and put a twenty pound turkey with stuffing in it in the oven. While that was baking she made the dressing and a jello salad.

The table was groaning with turkey with stuffing and dressing, ham, fried chicken, corn on the cob, potato salad, pickled beets, deviled eggs, coleslaw, squash and green beans. The yeast rolls with homemade butter were delicious. There was bread pudding, the Banana Split cake, jello, coconut cake, banana pudding and the cookies. Hot cider, buttermilk, sweet milk, coffee and water were offered.

After Joshua asked a blessing, they all ate as if they had not eaten for days. Charity had announced, "Sitz and eat yourself full," and they took her at her word.

The Kimes brought pecan pies and apple pies. All of this was quickly devoured. The children ran out to play marbles, jump rope and tag. The men settled with coffee to talk while the women cleaned up.

Charity took Alicia aside to talk to her about rumspringa. Alicia would soon be eighteen and maybe she would have a boyfriend and do all that she wanted to do. The next year she could participate in rumspringa which was a year in which the young people could do as the English did and could even go outside their community and live as the English. They had a free choice then of staying outside and living as English or joining the church and be baptized. If they choose to live outside they could never live at home again. The family would have to give them up. If at any time they came back and asked the church to forgive them and allow them to be baptized, they would be welcomed. Alicia was older and shy.

Even though she missed her mother, Charity was relieved that the Thanksgiving dinner went so well and that her daed was settling down. She knew his heart was still hurting because he and Jenna Mae had married for love and had remained faithful all through the years.

Now she had to start planning for Christmas and all the gifts she would make. There would be a long list of relatives and friends. The Amish did not put much thought into special Christmas gifts. They felt the time should be given to remembering the birth of Jesus and what He had meant to the world. They knew it was not His actual birth date, but it is a remembrance of Him.

Joshua and Jacob had taken time to teach Jeremiah how to take care of his horse. He squatted down and got in everyone's way trying to see how the farrier trimmed hooves. Joshua put Jeremiah on one of his horses to start training him how to ride properly and care for his horse before and after the ride.

Christmas Eve with snow on the ground. Some child in school had told Jeremiah that at midnight the animals would talk and praise God. He was determined to stay up and go to the barn to see for himself. Charity had a difficult time convincing him that it was just a story. He fell asleep on the living room couch any way. He was getting too heavy for her to carry so she left him there.

"Mamm! You let me sleep through the animals talking and now I will never get to hear them."

"Never Jeremiah? Are you saying you will not live any more?" she teased him.

He grinned. "Aww, you know what I mean."

"Yes, I know my darling, little man. Now we must do our chores, have breakfast and prepare for church. We always have a Christmas service."

"We go every Christmas and they say the same things. How Jesus was born and why we should worship him. Can we stay at home today? I would rather go sledding or ice skating on the river."

"Oh, Jeremiah. Your daed would be so disappointed in you if he could hear you say that. He loved to go to church and learn about Jesus."

"But he is not here to listen to me. I do not want to go to church."

"Jeremiah, I would fail as a good mother if I did not take you to church and help you to learn how to be a good Amish Christian. Grossmudder Leah, and the Grossfadders will be expecting to see you, not to mention all your uncles and aunts."

"You are going to make me go I know."

"Make you? I hope you will be man enough to go without me having to make you."

"Oh, all right," he gruffed, kicking his shoe on the floor and then against the stove. "We need to do our chores."

"We sure do," she answered cheerfully as she grabbed a shawl to put over her head and shoulders. "Let us go."

Jeremiah was right. The pastors read the story in Luke. They had sung and had several prayers. Jeremiah was beginning to wiggle when the final prayer was said.

"Come on, Jerry," Charity was surprised to hear Mark Hershberger call.

He was gone before she could stop him. She sighed and went to the kitchen to help the women prepare the noon meal.

Back at home, Charity asked her son. "Did I hear Mark call you Jerry?"

"Ja mamm. That is what I am called at school and I like it."

"Did you remind them that your name is Jeremiah, not Jerry."

"They know. I like to be called Jerry because it makes me feel like one of the big boys."

Charity could see she would loose the so-called battle, so she stopped talking about it. She knew her son would rather fit in with the rest of the children, and she did understand.

Jeremiah had brought her a profile shadow picture of him that had been made at school. She made him special shirt and pants to be worn while he was learning to ride in Joshua's indoor ring.

In the past Joshua and Adam had planned on raising horses and training them. They had built the indoor ring so they could work in any kind of weather.

Noah Kime had sent word to Matthew that his cow would give birth just any time. If he wanted to bring Jeremiah, he would be welcome. Matthew talked to Charity who did not like the idea.

"Sister dear. All farm children learn about the mating of animals and birth. Jeremiah is certainly old enough to see for himself. If Adam were here, he would have given him the chance before now. You hover over him too much. I know why you do it. Because you miss Adam and he is of Adam's blood. You can not protect him all his life from knowing the good and the bad in the world. We need to give him the experience and be with him to show him what is right and wrong."

Charity could not answer him because she was trying very hard to keep from crying. Finally she spoke. "My head tells me you are right, bruder, but my heart wants to keep him my little boy as long as possible."

He hugged her. "I know schwesechder. Your big bruder understands. Believe me, I know how you feel, but you must allow him room to grow or he will resent you and maybe become a big problem."

"What do you mean a big problem?" she asked worriedly.

"Resenting Amish rules. Getting into all kinds of trouble. Maybe even making the decision to leave home when he is in rumspringa."

"He would never do that. He knows how much I love him."

"You keep treating him like a baby and he will resent it."

She sighed deeply. "All right. I do not like it, but take him if you will."

Jeremiah was so excited that he kept bouncing on his seat and talking fast and loudly. "How will we know when the baby cow will be here? Will I get to see it being brought in?"

"Settle down, Jeremiah. You will frighten my horses and cause them to run away with us. I know you would think it is exciting, but we might wreck and hurt the horses or hurt us. Yes, you will get to see the calf being born."

"Why do you keep saying being born, oom Matthew? The doctor brings the baby cow to the mother I think."

Matthew laughed. "You will soon know. I hope you do not get sick. Your mamm would be angry with me."

"Why would I get sick?"

"Stop asking so many questions. I know you are excited, but you will soon know."

When they pulled in to great oom Noah's barn lot, Jeremiah jumped down ready to run into the barn.

"Jeremiah!" Matthew spoke sharply. "Wait on me. The mother cow might get frightened at you running in. She does not know you and she might think you will do her some harm."

"But I will not hurt her, and I want to see."

"You can see. Remember, talk softly and do not run. We do not want to upset the mother cow."

Jeremiah crowded in the stall door between Noah and Matthew. "Who is he?" he asked in a whisper.

"Shhh. That is Doctor Retstatt. He is going to help the mother have her baby."

Jeremish was so excited, he forgot to be quiet. "Where is the baby? He is not holding one that I can see."

Noah squatted down beside Jeremiah to explain. "The baby is in the mother's stomach. When God is ready for it to be born, He will bring the baby out."

Matthew shook his head. "Charity has not done the right thing keeping him from learning about the farm animals."

Suddenly the cow gave a mooo of pain. Jeremiah nearly jumped out of his skin. "What is wrong? She sounds like she is hurting."

"She is hurting. Be very quiet and step in with me beside this stall wall and look what the doctor is doing." Noah took Jeremiah's hand and stepped inside the stall with him.

With round eyes Jeremiah looked at the cow with her sides heaving and straining. Suddenly a sack burst out of her and blood and fluids gushed out.

Jeremiah grabbed Noah's leg and held on tightly. As the calf started to be born, he shook as if he were scared stiff.

"What is that? What is wrong?"

"Shh. That is the baby calf being born. It is time for it to come out of the mother's stomach now."

Jeremiah felt very sick. He could hardly stand it. He was itching, sweating and breathing fast. "Do people babies come out like that? Did I come out of mamm like that?"

"Yes, Jeremiah, you did."

"Did mamm cry out in pain like that?"

"She probably did."

Jeremiah turned and started to run. Matthew caught up with him. 'Where are you going?"

"Let go of me. I am going home. I have to. I need to see mamm."

Matthew picked him up under one arm like a sack and thanked Noah for allowing them to visit. He took Jeremiah out to the buggy and sat him up on the seat. Jeremiah was shaking and looking white. Matthew was afraid he was going to be sick.

CHAPTER NINE

In Charity's back yard, Jeremiah jumped down from the buggy before Matthew could stop and tie the horse. He ran into the back door.

"Mamm! Mamm!"

She came running. "What? What is it, Jeremiah?" By then Matthew was in the kitchen, also.

Jeremiah ran and grabbed her around the waist and buried his head in her apron. He started to sob.

Charity looked helplessly at Matthew who explained. "I guess it was a shock for him. He expected to see the veterinarian carry a baby in."

Charity was angry. "I told all of you that he was not ready. Now see what you have done."

"No, sister dear. See what you have done. He is going on eight and most farm children by the age of five have seen animals mating and births. You have hovered over him too much."

Jeremiah turned his tear-drenched face up to his mother. "Mamm, I am so sorry."

"What are you sorry about my little man?"

"I am sorry you did all that so you could have me. I did not know you carried me in your stomach. Is that why tante Deborah got so big? Was Jenna Louise in her stomach?"

"Yes, all babies are in the mother's stomach until God decides when it is time for them to be born."

"So that is what being born means." He turned quickly. "Oom Matthew, would you like to play a game of checkers with me?"

Relieved, Matthew agreed to play one game and then he had to go do his evening chores. Charity was relieved that he was not asking more about babies being born. She dreaded the time when he would ask how the baby got in the mother's stomach.

In January the snow had left the ground, but it was still very cold. Joshua and Jacob decided that this was a good time to build the extra rooms on the store. They measured and found there was space enough for three average rooms and one bigger one. The bigger one would be for Jacob to build furniture and show it. In the space left, Charity asked for an indoor bathroom. She was tired of running to the restaurant down the street, and she did have customers who might like to use a restroom. She was not going to ask the Bishop's permission.

Joshua had casually mentioned, after church, that they would be building. on Monday and for none of them expect to hear from him or Jacob for several days.

Monday morning they got up at their usual five o' clock and did their chores. Jacob left his three in charge. Lawrence would help some. Matthew had too much work of his own, and Deborah needed him with a new baby.

By the time Charity opened the store at eight, Jacob, Joshua and Lawrence were there with the huge stack of pressure-treated lumber. They were prepared to set the sides and prop up boards so the concrete could be poured as soon as they mixed it.

Much to their surprise Sheriff Micah Fleming pulled up in a van and let eight Amish men, with tool belts on, out of the van. He explained that they had not wanted to park horses and buggies on Main Street all day, so he had brought them to help with the building.

Their attention turned to a big truck with a rolling vat behind it. David Bolling had brought a vat full of mixed cement to help out. His construction business could wait a day or two because he wanted to help Charity, also.

The men were relieved and thankful to get the cement because it saved them from mixing for half a day in wheelbarrows with hoes and shovels.

They quickly set up the frames for the various rooms under the direction of Jacob. By noon they were ready to pour the cement and then it had to set a couple of days before the building could be completed.

By now Charity was becoming excited thinking her store was going to be nice like the one in Shipshewana. It would not be as large as the Yoder store, but it would be all the Bishop would give her permission to have.

Charity, and the ladies working with her, were willing to put up with the noises of hammering and banging as the men worked. A few additional men had come in to help, English included.

David Bolling insisted on donating the window glass and helping all he could. Dr. Alicea had come by, as often as possible, to make sure his services were not needed. Pete Mulanaugh brought tasty snacks for everyone each day from his restaurant. Jim & Anita Bledsoe came by and offered to help Charity carry and arrange supplies. They were warmly welcomed; the Amish remembered that Jim was hurt and hospitalized coming to their aid in the fight when the boys from town jumped on the Amish boys. Anita had made an excellent witness for them in the court hearing. (Read in *Amish Dilemma*) They were sincerely thanked and told the Amish men would carry the loads for Charity.

With so much good help and the weather cooperating, cold but clear, the work was completed in a week. Jacob brought in a few pieces of furniture that he had been working on at home.

Charity walked through the entire store and drew a breath of pride and gratitude. She didn't forget to thank God for these blessings and to ask His forgiveness for taking pride in her store. Everyone assured her that it was all right considering all she had been through and what was now done.

The porch had been extended across the entire front of the building. The windows facing the porch had been built out in window boxes. The first room, entering the store, was the old part and still had a lot of the same supplies in it. To the left was an open area where the finished furniture would be displayed. All Amish men, who built furniture, were welcome to build and display their work and then to pay Charity a small commission.

Behind the display area was a big room for making the furniture. Beside this was the bathroom Charity had wanted. To the right, of the old store, was the old storage room with a cot in it for resting. Here were stored lanterns, kerosene, leather goods and anything needed on the farm.

To the left of the storage room was the work room for the women who would quilt and sew. Two quilting frames hung from the ceiling and the two peddle sewing machines were in this room. Going past the quilting room was the sewing needs such as threads, yarns, crochet thread, needles of all shapes and sizes, scissors, small individual quilting frames and anything connected with sewing, knitting and crocheting including bolts of cloth, lace and anything that one could want.

To the left through this room was a beautiful room with a hand-made bed with lovely hand-made quilts and pillows and a feather mattress. There was a hand-made dining table with eight chairs. This was covered with a beautiful hand-embroidered cloth with a lovely setting of dishes, goblets and tableware. There were flat windows in each of the back rooms.

On the front porch were four hand-made rockers. Two on each side. On the left a round hand-made table set between the two rockers. The same size table set between the two rockers on the opposite side. These were brought in each night and placed out again each morning. People were encouraged to purchase pastries or snacks and a cold soda, or a hot drink, and set on the front porch eating, talking and gently rocking.

Charity threw her arms around her daddy. This was not an action that an Amish woman took, but Charity not only loved her daddy, but was very grateful for his caring and help. She then turned and hugged Joshua, her father-in-law, whom she loved dearly. She thanked all the men who had worked to make this possible. She was very grateful and thankful to God for His blessings and giving these men the skill to do the work and want to help her.

Rosemary suggested that Charity might want to have an open house afternoon and invite everyone in to see the improvements. It would be good for business and they could make snacks to serve. Jacob suggested that she talk to the Bishop about it and get his approval. He could see nothing wrong with it, but one never knew how the Bishop and the church would look at it.

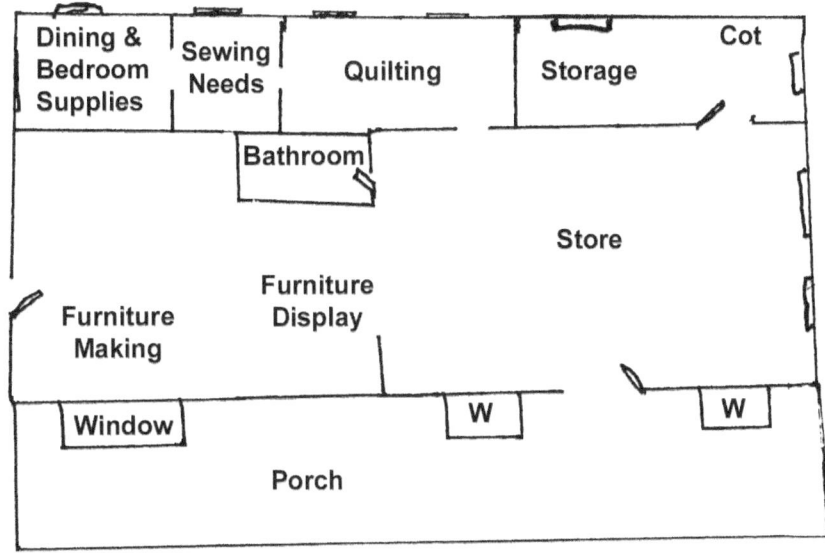

Drawing of Charity's Store

The following Sunday the church service was held in the home of Bishop Yoder. Charity went early for the purpose of talking to him about a special time to invite the public in to see her new store. The Bishop discussed it with the pastors and the deacon. They approved, so he asked the deacon to give the information to the congregation and ask for their opinions.

Charity waited impatiently for the meeting. She was saying a silent prayer the entire time that she waited and knew Rosemary and the others, who worked for her, were doing the same. Finally the deacon stood up and told of Charity's request and asked for opinions.

Everyone loved Charity and the family. They knew how hard the young widow had worked and she had not done anything disgraceful to the Amish beliefs. She was respected and admired. They seemed to all agree that it would be good for her business and bring the name of Amish furniture makers to the public in addition to the sewing and quilting.

Charity was humbled at the comments and thanked everyone sincerely. She told the ladies that she would teach them how to use the peddle sewing machines and let them work in her store. She would pay everyone who worked and if any of the women had quilts, or sewing of any kind, that they wanted to sell, she would allow them to sell it in her store for a small fee.

One of the teenagers in rumspringa jumped up, which was unheard of in Amish meetings. "Would you let us put up a sign that we can be hired? We need to make some money for ourselves, and I know a boy who needs to work to help his widowed mother."

Charity's heart was touched and without waiting for the church's approval declared that she would do whatever she could to help. The Bishop quickly got order and turned the meeting over to the song leader and then the pastors.

Charity had hired three additional Amish girls and two English to work in her store. She brought everyone together and discussed what day would be most suitable for them for an opening and what they could serve.

They decided to have it all day on a Saturday, although they did not usually work on a Saturday. The Saturday coming up was a day before the Sunday with no church service. This would be more reasonable to the Amish community.

They agreed to serve Amish Nut Brittle, slices of Friendship Bread with butter and jam, Amish Apple Dumplings, Amish Christmas Cookies and Amish Whoopie Pies. (The recipe for Whoopie Pies, and Friendship Bread can be found in *Amish Dilemma*. The others are in this book at the back.)

Most of the women did not care to be paid for quilting and sewing. They were pleased to be out with friends and doing something different. They were all proud, even though they could not admit it, of their tiny stitches and neat sewing. The rumor has gone around that there is always a defect in a quilt or garment because it would be worldly to be perfect. I personally do not understand how this could be true. Everything is too well made.

The women loved learning to make blouses, skirts, dresses and slacks for the English. The work was so different, but satisfying. Some even made gloves, matching purses and hats.

All of the work progressed better than had been expected. Several women came in just to visit and quilt. They also brought items to be sold, especially baby clothes, candies, candles and other decorating items. A few of the women had learned to make the fancy candles with the carvings on them. A few brought their knitting to display and sell.

On Friday, even though in the past they had closed early, a half dozen women were kept busy all day making the items that would be offered to be eaten. They laughed and shared stories about themselves learning to cook and care for a new husband.

When Joshua came in with Jeremiah, Charity suddenly realized she had been too busy all week to do more than the basic essentials with her precious son. She ran to hug him which embarrassed him in front of the others. He proudly showed her the book in which he had completed third grade Math and received an A on the assignments. He was reminded by several of the women to not be proud. He privately thought he could not help it.

Joshua had come to take Charity home. He was concerned about the late hour and the threatening storm. On the way home thunder suddenly rolled in sonic blasts frightening the big draft horse. The big, old trees swayed in the vicious wind as blinding lightening ripped across the sky.

Charity was pleased and thankful to find that Matthew, Maeve and Joseph had fed all the animals, gathered the eggs and had done her chores. Maeve was still in the kitchen and had a kettle of hot chocolate ready to break the chill for her family members and Joshua.

Joshua hurriedly drank a cup of hot chocolate and went to take his horse home just as rain and sleet mixed began to fall. He predicted that they would have snow over the weekend. Charity was concerned about her open house the next day.

That night wind whistled around the house adding a ghostly wail to the thunder and lightning. The sleet, crashing against her bedroom window like marbles being thrown against it, was oddly rhythmic. She was lying awake when Jeremiah ran into her room and jumped into bed with her.

"Mamm, there is just too much noise. I can't sleep and thought you might need some comfort."

"Danki, my darling zoon. It is so thoughtful of you to think of your old mamm, and want to comfort me. I think I can sleep now." She gathered his flannel-clad body in a sweet hug and both went to sleep.

CHAPTER TEN

Saturday morning Charity was relieved to see the storm had passed over and the day apparently was going to be clear. She smiled at the figure of her son scooted down half-way in the bed under the quilts. How was he breathing? She decided to leave him in his comfort and go about her chores.

It was five twenty when Charity walked out her back door to go to the barn. She met her baby brother, Joseph, coming with a bucket full of milk. She hugged him and told him how much she appreciated him. He had fed all the animals and milked the cow, but the eggs were still to be gathered and the chickens fed. She took care of that and then ran in to get a big breakfast for them.

Jeremiah wandered sleepily in and scolded her for not getting him up to help with the work. He was delighted to see Joseph. Charity made oatmeal for them. While Joseph and Jeremiah ate, Charity made their favorite pancakes and put a bowl of applesauce on the table. She had served coffee and milk to her two boys and now poured a second cup of coffee for Joseph and herself. Jeremiah loved her pancakes. There was fresh churned butter on the table with fresh caught maple syrup. She had helped stir the sap.

She hurriedly cleaned the kitchen and made the beds. By seven thirty Joseph left to go home and take Jeremiah with him. Jeremiah protested all morning that he had never seen an open house and wanted to go with his mother. Charity and Joseph both told him it only meant that all people were invited to come in and see her new store and maybe they would trade with her.

He left kicking the dirt and refusing to hold Joseph's hand. There had been so much rain during the night that Charity knew he was getting a lot of mud on his boots. She knew he would have to remove his boots and clean them before going in the house.

Rosemary's younger brother, David, was in rumspringa and was driving a car. He had offered to come take Charity to the store and she gladly accepted. By ten until eight they were at the store. Rosemary had a key and had already opened. All of the workers were present including Lisa Kennedy. She was so grateful to Charity for giving her a chance to prove her worth as a friend and worker.

A group of Amish came in first eager to see all that the Bishop had approved. They were amazed that there was electricity and a bathroom in an Amish store. There was even a telephone, but it was only for business.

Some town people came in a little later followed by tourists and more town people. Everyone thought the food was delicious and bought some to take home with them. Some of the women were kept busy preparing more food.

The two English women, working in the sewing room, showed catalogues of clothes they could make to the town people. The Amish women took measurements and allowed the buyer to select her own cloth for the clothes. Some of the English selected embroidery items to be appliquéd on the cloth.

A few larger women were thrilled to get this special service. It was difficult for them to buy from a store and still obtain style and looks. They all made appointments to return and pay for the clothes.

The tourists were thrilled to see the hand-made furniture, the faceless dolls and the fancy candles. Some furniture sold and arrangements were made for shipping. They also asked for her card to share with friends back home. Charity had to quickly write this information out and a note to herself to get some cards made. She knew it would probably be considered worldly, but she would only use them strictly in a business opportunity.

Charity and her workers took turns going into the storage room to quickly eat a sandwich and drink coffee or a soda. She tried not to take much time because she wanted her workers to have a rest and a chance to eat.

As she stepped out of the room a deep voice behind her said, "Finally, I caught you." She whirled, ready to scream, with her heart fluttering and found herself hugged by Dr. Isaac Yoder. She quickly stepped back because she did not want the Amish to report her to the Bishop.

"Dr. Yoder!" she exclaimed. "What a nice surprise and how wonderful to see you. What brings you all the way here?"

"Dear lady, I came especially to see you. I'm in the area on business and happened to hear of your wonderful success, and I just had to come and help you celebrate."

"I am so happy you came by. Friends, I want you to meet the wonderful doctor who took care of me when I was in the hospital in Shipshewana. This is the marvelous Dr. Yoder."

"You were in the hospital when you went to Shipshewana!" She had not told everyone of her horrendous experience.

"Yes," Dr. Yoder continued, "three hoodlums decided to make a punching bag of her and try to take advantage of her, but two former football players took them out of commission. She was taken to the hospital where I worked for bruises and trauma."

"Mamm! Some bad men hurt you? You did not tell me. Why did not you let me go with you? I would have beat them up for you. I do not want anyone hurting my sweet mamm."

"Jeremiah! What are you doing here? Did Joseph bring you?"

"No. I am big enough to come by myself. I walked and ranned."

"You ran. For shame. You ran off and they are all probably looking for you and getting so worried. How could you shame me like that?"

"I am sorry, but I have never seen an open house and you would not let me come."

"You can see for yourself that it is nothing unusual. It is just people shopping."

Isaac Yoder could not contain his laughter. "I assume this is your offspring. Determined and independent just like you," he laughed.

"Yes, this is my disobedient Jeremiah. Jeremiah, this is the nice Dr. Yoder who took care of me in the hospital."

"I am pleased to meet you, Dr. Yoder," he said with a handshake. Charity was proud of him for being a gentleman, but he did disobey.

Joseph ran in the door out of breath. "Charity, Charity. I am sorry to bother you, but Jeremiah ran away and I can not ----. There you are. Ooh, I am going to give it to you for scaring us like that."

"Jeremiah, go on home now with Joseph and we will talk about this when I get home."

"Can I have some cookies?"

"May I? And no you may not. Little boys who do not mind are not given cookies. Now go on and stay at home." Joseph left holding on to the struggling Jeremiah.

"Well, may I have a cookie and may I look over your store?" Isaac Yoder grinned.

"You may have whatever you wish and yes, you may look to your heart's content. I am pleased with what we have." She took him around showing him what her men folks and friends had done. He was impressed with the furniture, the quilting and the food.

"I would like to place an order for furniture in my new office."

"Certainly, Dr. Yoder. Of course you will want it shipped as soon as possible."

"Oh, no. Only delivered across town."

What?! You are going to practice here with us now?"

"I completed my term, and more, that the Bishop ask me to serve. Remember, I told you I wanted to go to a smaller community. Well, here I am. I have purchased Dr. Goodley's business and goodwill in the hospital."

"I did hear that Dr. Goodley was elderly and not well. He has served us faithfully for many years. Even though he is English, he has treated the Amish with all his skill and caring. We appreciate him, but you will certainly be welcomed. Why did you choose our little community?"

"You are responsible for that."

"Me!"

"Yes, you. I was attracted to my lovely patient and wanted to get better acquainted. With your permission, I would like to visit you and give us a chance to know each other better. Too, your little son will need time to learn to share you with someone else."

"I do not know what to say," she said feeling very warm.

"Don't say anything yet. Just think about it. There is no hurry. I am not going to rush you."

"But my dear Adam is still in my heart. I have not even thought of another man in my personal life. My brothers, father, father-in-law and friends have filled that empty space very well."

"That is why I don't want to rush you. From what I hear, I would have sincerely liked and admired your Adam. He will always have a place in your heart. But isn't your heart big enough to hold me, too?"

"I have not had a single thought about another man. I do like you and admire you for your kind nature and work ethics. Give me time to think."

"That is what I intend to do. Now if I may buy some of the delicious bread, fruit and pastries, I shall be on my way. I'm looking for a house. At the present I'm staying in

Nissley's B & B. May I come visit you at home soon and let Jeremiah get acquainted with me?

Charity was feeling **very** warm. "I -- I guess that would be all right. I need to talk to my family about this. You know my mother died just a few months ago and my daed is still grieving."

"Me coming to see you will not hurt him. Charity, I am sure he would say that we should take our time and get better acquainted."

"All right, Dr. Yoder. We will let time decide."

"Don't you think you could call me Isaac now?"

She blushed and smiled. "Maybe."

They said their good nights and Charity turned to speak to others who were leaving. She checked the store but her good workers had already cleaned up and had the store ready to close. She thanked them sincerely and bid them all a good night.

She decided to walk out on the sidewalk and wait on whoever was coming to pick her up. As she passed the grocery store, a jewelry store was next. Suddenly men rushed out of the jewelry store, guns were fired and the police were there as the men ran for a black sedan.

Charity threw herself down on the sidewalk trying to make as small a target as possible. The men ran for the car, jumped out ran in all directions instead. The police were right after them. An ambulance came up and the attendants ran into the jewelry store. They came out carrying the owner, Dan Moody, on a stretcher.

The police came back with the three men they had captured. One officer ran to help Charity up. "Are you all right miss? Are you hurt?"

"Thank you, no. I am fine. I put myself down there so I would not be shot. Do you have the men who committed this crime?"

"Yes, all three of them are in custody."

"Three? Are you sure there were only three?"

"Why do you ask?"

"Look at the car. All four doors are open. Why would just three men open all four doors trying to get back in the car?"

He looked stunned. "Hey buddies. I'm afraid we still have one at large. This nice lady just pointed out that all four doors are open, but we have only three men. Spread out. We can't let an armed man, wanted by the law, run loose in the town among innocent people."

The three men in handcuffs were taken to the jail to be booked and charged. Four other officers began to walk the streets looking down every alley and behind every closed store. After an hour they gave up.

"He has probably run into the residential neighborhood, "the sergeant in charge stated. "We need to go to every door and check to make sure he isn't in a house holding hostages. We also need to warn the people to keep doors locked and call us if they are suspicious of anything."

He turned to Charity. "Thank you, Miss, for being so alert. Do you need one of us to walk home with you?"

At that moment Jacob came driving a horse and buggy.

"Thank you, but my father is here to take me home."

"You people don't have guns do you?"

"Only rifles or shotguns for hunting. We do not believe in firing at a person."

"You may have to if he tries to enter one of your homes." He then told Jacob what had transpired and cautioned him to be on the alert going home.

"Do you want us to follow you and make sure you get home safely?"

"Nee, danki," Jacob answered. "God is with us."

"That won't keep the man from shooting you if he thinks you're in his way."

Jacob smiled and spoke softly, "Cast your cares on the Lord and He will sustain you. He will never let the righteous fall, but, You, oh God, will bring down the wicked." (Psalm 55:22-23)

The officer stood with open mouth, took a deep breath and nodded. "I guess you're protected then. Get home safely and have a nice night."

Jacob clucked to the horse and headed to Charity's home. The officer shook his head and walked over to tell the others what Jacob had said.

"He makes me believe," he said reverently. They continued to search.

"Danki, daed," Charity said sincerely as she went into her house and Jacob headed home. Jeremiah was still at Jacob's house with Joseph and would spend the night. Since there was no church service the next day, Charity decided to leave him.

She felt uneasy and looked all over her house to make sure no one was in there that did not belong. She cleaned up, said her prayers, but did not read the Bible. Her sleep was restless that night.

Charity walked over to Jacob's house. Jeremiah hurried to hug his mother and talk excitedly about his day, hoping she would forget to scold him for running away. Joseph did not let her forget and she had not.

Jacob spoke sternly to Jeremiah. "You worried all of us yesterday and we had to stop our necessary work and look for you. I think your mamm needs to start spanking you."

Charity cried out, "Oh, I could not do that. He looks just like Adam and I love them both so much."

"Dochder, God will not think you have been a good mother. We are to discipline with love. How is he going to remember to think before he acts if you do not guide him in that direction?"

"He is still a little boy. When he gets older he will know right from wrong. We are all teaching him. He will learn to think before he acts."

"But he does not fear the result of his actions, and he must for his own sake. He might make the wrong decision before he's old enough to know the difference and put himself in danger. How would you feel then?"

"I know what you are saying, but I can not spank him."

Jeremiah breathed a sigh of relief until Joseph spoke. "I suggest you take something from him that he really loves and make him think about it."

Jacob put his arm across Jeremiah's shoulders. "I am not going to let you near your horse or take a riding lesson for two weeks. You will stay at home, except for school, and you will help your mamm."

Charity was almost in tears for him, but she knew her father and brother were right in their thinking. She meekly took Jeremiah by the hand and went home.

Jeremiah ran in the house and got his bat and ball. "Let me have that, Jeremiah. I want you to sit down and write about running away yesterday and how you feel about it now."

He started to whine, but Charity looked so sternly at him that he quietly went to his room and got his paper and pencil. He sat down at his desk that Jacob had made for him and started thinking about what to write.

CHAPTER ELEVEN

Charity had spent a restless night, tossing and turning. She worried knowing that she should be more strict with Jeremiah, but her heart would not allow it. She still had a deep love for Adam and Jeremiah came from him. She loved them both more than she could explain.

Wearily she got up to start the day. First getting Jeremiah up so that he could help with the chores. Then while he cleaned up and dressed, she got breakfast for them.

Monday Marilyn came by for Jeremiah. He hurried out before his mother could give him a lecture and before she might tell Marilyn how disobedient he had been. He waved gaily at her as they went off at a crisp pace.

It was early but Charity decided to go on to the store and get there ahead of the others. She decided to ride the gentle work horse this morning and one of her brothers would come to take him back home.

With a joyful heart she stepped into the store and looked around with a great feeling of accomplishment. Open house had been a tremendous success and she had made new friends. Her mind wandered briefly to the robbery at the jewelry store and then put it out of her mind. It had nothing to do with her.

Why did the store seem so cold even with the heat on? Wandering back to the quilting room she discovered that the window had been broken large enough for a person to crawl through. The latch was still engaged.

She should have turned then and run for help, but she walked closer to the window. A stinking body came up behind her and a dirty hand came over her mouth and nose. Struggling for breath, she didn't think to fight. It was not the Amish way. For a second she wished she knew how to fight this person.

"Keep quiet and I'll take my hand down." She nodded her head. His hand slipped down but still held her arms. She could not see who it was.

"Who are you and what do you want?" she spoke shakily. "I do not bother anyone else and expect everyone to show me the same respect."

"Now why does that sound familiar? Oh, yes. In Shipshewana you told me and my buddies to mind our own business just as you were minding yours."

"Shipshewana! Were you one of the men who attacked me? What are you doing here?"

"Just lucky I guess. We needed money and meant to take it from the jewelry store and move on out of town. You, with your nosey nose noticed the fourth door being opened and caused the police to hunt for me. I would have gotten clean away if it weren't for you."

"I don't understand. How did you get here where I live?"

"We just came this way thinking to head to New York and get lost in a big city. It was just by accident that our car decided to give us trouble when we got here. We might even have gone into Canada."

"What are you going to do now?" *I hope you leave for Canada.*

"Well how about I finish what we started in Shipshewana?"

"I don't understand. You put me in the hospital there by treating me so roughly. I don't know what else you can do. Are you going to beat me up again?"

He laughed harshly. "Are you as innocent as you pretend to be or are you just killing time until your workers arrive and help you?"

"They will be here any minute. Please do not hurt any of them. Why will you not just go and I will not tell anyone you were here."

"Oh yeah. Fat chance of that."

Just then she heard the front door open. "Don't open your mouth or I'll kill all of them," he snarled as he pulled a pistol from the small of his back.

There was complete silence and she wondered why there was no talking or moving around.

He was nervous and, placing his body very close to her back, he walked her to the front. She was surprised. There was no one and no noise.

"*%#* I could have sworn I heard the door open. Isn't it time for your workers to come in. Ah there," he said as two Amish women walked to the front door.

Just then a deep voice spoke from behind him. "Drop your gun and don't turn around. Leave the woman alone."

He felt the point of a gun against the back of his neck. "I can shot and not kill you, but you would be paralyzed from the neck down for the rest of your life. As far as I'm concerned that would be the best prison for you. Now drop the gun, put your hands behind your neck and drop to your knees."

At that moment the Zook twins walked in and screamed. Men, passing on the sidewalk, ran in to see what the trouble was. They smiled at the man behind who was holding two guns in his hand. A scruffy, dirty man was on his knees with his hands behind his neck. He tried to take advantage of the situation and jumped up to run toward the door. Charity stuck her foot out and tripped him. He went down face first and was handcuffed.

She turned to see a tall, copper-skinned young man in western clothes and wearing a badge. She stared at the unexpected sight of this man.

"Yes, I'm Shawnee Indian, but I'm also a U. S. Marshal. We've been after these characters all across the United States for robbery, rape and murder, arson and you name it."

"How - how did you get in here. I heard the door open, but there was no one there."

At that moment Rosemary, Lisa and two other ladies came out of the storeroom where they had been hiding. Rosemary explained.

"When we came through the front door this man came to us and introduced himself as a U. S. Marshal. He explained that he thought the criminal was in the store and he had seen you go in. He asked us to tiptoe and hide, which we did."

Charity turned to the Marshal. "How did you think he might be in here?"

"By the way, my name is Richard Longbow. I was on the trail of these men and was on the walk when the three were captured. When the fourth got away, I stayed around to keep an eye open. Going around your building last night I saw the broken window, but not knowing when it was broken I wasn't sure if he had come in or not. I was just being cautious."

"I am so glad you were. My name is Charity Kime and this is my store. These men beat me and tried to rape me last fall in Shipshewana. Two former football players fought them and kept them for the police. I thought I would never see them again."

Richard grinned. "My mother says never say never. I'm sorry they found you and came here."

"According to him, they were not looking for me. It was by accident that they had car trouble and ended up here. Here is Sheriff Fleming."

Micah and Richard introduced themselves and Richard showed Micah his credentials. They agreed that Micah would take charge of the criminal.

Micah was so angry when he found that these were the men who roughed Charity up in Shipshewana, that he could hardly keep from beating the man.

Micah took the man on to jail and Richard stayed to look at Charity's store. He was impressed and wanted to buy something to take to his mother.

"Please select something and give me the privilege of mailing it to her. I do not know what I would have done if you had not been here to help me. Even if I knew how to fight him, I was too frightened." Charity was trembling, now that it was over.

"I don't expect anything from you. I was just doing my job and happy that I was here to help. Men, such as those, need to be put away for life. They are a blight on the whole nation. You say they were here by accident. I don't think that's the truth. It's too much to be coincidental."

Charity could not believe it of herself. Her stomach felt bubbly and effervescent. *I can not be attracted to this man. There will never be room in my heart for anyone else except Adam -- and of course, Jeremiah.*

"Please have a pastry and some hot cider. The girls will see that you are served. I can not thank you enough. Please excuse me. I need to call for a replacement for the broken window. If it rains in, the work might be harmed that the women are doing. There are quilts in both frames and a lot of cloth on the table where the women are cutting for clothes that have been ordered."

"I would love a pastry and a hot drink. Thank you."

The ladies snickered and giggled trying to please this handsome man. Christine Zook, who expected to get married in the fall, hurried to get him a platter of several of the pastries and a tall mug of hot cider. He did sit on the porch, in the chilly air, and rock contentedly as he rolled his eyes with pleasure at the taste of the pastries.

Charity called David Bolling and explained to him about the window. He promised he would have it in before the day was over. She hurried to meet some elderly Amish women who came to quilt and to tell them of the broken window. She was pleased that they all wanted to be together and share their joys and sorrows.

"Marian," Charity called to one of the English helpers, "please take a heater to the quilting room. The ladies may need some heat in there. Richard," she called to her new

Indian friend, "you are tall. Would you please tape this blanket over the window until the men can put in a new one? Thank you so much."

Richard gladly taped the blanket over the window and then turned to marvel at the beautiful colors and tiny stitches in the quilts. The older women would not look at his face, but kept their heads turned down to their sewing.

Amish women are not encouraged to talk or be too friendly with a man, especially if they are married. Charity was an exception. She had always been open and out-spoken. Adam had been forced to go to her defense against church men several times on her behalf. (See *Amish Dilemma*)

"Richard, where are you staying? I mean, are you in a motel or in a B & B?"

"No. I was right on the trail of the four men when they were caught breaking into the jewelry store. Then last night I walked the street and kept an eye on your building."

"That will never do. You probably have not eaten properly either. You must come home with me. I will feed you and you can stay the night."

The women gasped to hear this. Ninety year old Hester Eash was outraged. "Charity, you can not have a man in your house, and he is not even a relative. You will be meidung." She loved Charity and was honestly shocked and worried. She even forgot she was holding a needle and thread working on a quilt and stuck the needle down into her thigh. "Ouch!!"

"Oh, Hester, I am so sorry. I will not be shunned. I will have Jeremiah and my sister, Alicia. I am sure Lawrence will be checking in. It will be all right. Remember Hebrews 13:2 'Do not forget to entertain strangers, for by so doing some people have entertained angels'. No, Richard may not be a Heavenly angel, but he has been an angel to me." She smiled and hugged the dear, old lady.

"Charity, if it's going to cause trouble for you, I won't come to your house. I do respect that you are a widow and a single mother."

Martha Hartzler stood up from where she was quilting and came to Charity. "All our church members know what a good daughter, a good wife and a good mother you have been. If anyone says anything against you, my husband, Jedediah, and I will give them a tongue lashing."

It lightened the atmosphere in the room and everyone laughed thinking of the diminutive Martha threatening anyone. She barely stood five feet tall and probably weighed a hundred pounds.

Salome Bontrager clapped her hands. "This is not getting any work done and this **is** a place of business. Everyone, back to your work. And as for you, young man, we are thankful you were here for Charity. Gottes wille. Danki. Gott segeneich."

"What did she say?" Richard asked.

"She said it was God's will and thank you. She then said God bless you."

"What did she mean, it is God's will?"

"She meant everything is a purpose from God and it was God's will for you to be here when you were."

"How can I say thank you to her? I believe in God also."

Salome spoke, without turning around from her quilting, "Just be yourself. We all speak English."

Red-faced he followed the giggling Charity to the front. "I saw some beautifully carved candles back there. I've never seen anything like them. Would it be possible for you to wrap two of them for mailing to my mother?"

"I will gladly do so. Put your money away. I want to do this for your mother. She is a wonderful woman to raise such a fine, caring man. You didn't mention your father."

"He died when I was in high school. My mother worked very hard to make sure I finished school and attended college. She is worried about the job I have. My father and two uncles were in law enforcement and I've always admired them. I believe in justice being served and the innocent being protected. Too, I've been fortunate to catch some young teens before they got into real trouble and helped them turn their lives around."

"That is noble. I would like to hear more about your life. Are you married?"

"No. I have been too busy. I am on the go so much, and away from home, that it wouldn't be fair to a woman to leave her alone. And if there were children, she would have the sole responsibility of raising them."

"I love my son so much and do not regret having him. I have had help from my parents and my sisters and brothers, as well as the whole church family."

"If you're sure it's all right, I would appreciate your offer for a home-cooked meal and a bed for the night. I need to get back to Nevada tomorrow. I haven't yet talked to the authorities about the prisoners. I'm really supposed to take them into custody."

"Just relax here, or go to talk to the police about what you need to do. It will be another hour before I can leave. One of my bruders or my daed will come to take me home."

"Do you think they will mind me going with you?"

"It does not matter if they do. It is my house and my life. I am doing nothing wrong. The good Lord can see and know that."

He laughed. "Well I don't want to get you into trouble."

"You will not. Now go on."

CHAPTER TWELVE

The store stayed busy right until closing time. Gossip spreads faster than the wind and people had heard about the break-in and the arrest. There were several just looking, but most of them purchased something. One English couple purchased a full bedroom set that Jacob had made. Charity was thrilled for him, and for her store. Word would be spread and others would come in to look and buy.

A half hour before closing, Aaron Perkins, who worked for David Bolling, came in and installed a new window. He refused payment, so Charity gave him two loaves of bread and some ham to take with him. She was very firm in not taking charity.

Richard was back just as she was closing. They only stood a minute or two talking when Joseph came with his prize high-stepping Hanoverian pulling the carriage. Jeremiah was with him.

Jeremiah hopped off the carriage with bug eyes looking at Richard.

"Who are you?"

"Jeremiah. Do not be rude. I am going to introduce you. Joseph, this is Richard Longbow. He came to my aid this morning and captured the fourth criminal. I am taking him home for the night. Joseph is my youngest brother and going into rumspringa. This is my disobedient son, Jeremiah."

"Joseph, I am pleased to make your acquaintance. I've heard so much about Charity's family. Hello, disobedient son. You are not really are you?"

"Yes, I am her son. I am the man of the house and take care of my mamm," he answered with his chin stuck out as if he were ready to fight.

"No, I know you're her son. What I meant was, are you really disobedient? You don't look like a boy who would be."

Jeremiah hung his head and did not answer. Joseph laughed. "Get in the carriage. It would take a week to tell you all he has done that he should not have."

Joseph was courteous but he couldn't keep from worry about his sister taking this man home with her. What would the church think? He knew she was a righteous woman, but Amish, especially women, were expected to conduct themselves above reproach.

"Are you truly a real Indian?" Jeremiah asked when they were in the house and Charity was preparing supper.

"Jeremiah, do not be rude."

"Oh, that's okay. He isn't being rude, just curious as all little boys are. Yes, I'm a full blooded Indian, a Shawnee. My father and mother are both Indian and I grew up on a reservation."

"Where is your bow and arrow, your tomahawk and feather head piece?"

"Jeremiah, that is still being rude, and how did you know about all that anyway. I know you do not study it in school."

"That is something else. Tell your mamm, Jeremiah, where you have been sneaking off to after school. He thinks he is in rumspringa already. We warned you about not disciplining him."

Richard broke in. "Excuse me for intruding, but what is this rum thing you keep talking about?"

They took a few minutes to tell him of the year that seventeen to twenty year old Amish youth have the privilege of living as the English do. If they decide to stay away and be English, they are no longer welcome in the church or community. They are not baptized until they come to the church and ask to be baptized and taken as a church member. That only happens when they are old enough to understand what they are doing and what baptism really means.

"Now, my dear son. I have not forgotten. What are you doing after school?"

"Nothing," he mumbled and hung his head.

"Jeremiah, tell the truth. You want to be the man of the house, then act like one," Joseph told him.

"All right," he said defiantly, "sometimes, not every day, but sometimes I go into the sports bar and play pool and watch television."

"And they let you in?" Charity gasped. "Surely they can see you are too young."

"Jimmy Monroe and I walk down the alley and go in the back door. The men that are playing pool, in the back room, think it is all right for us to play. They ask me a lot of questions about Amish and I tell them the truth."

"What do they say?" Richard asked.

"Not much. They mostly just laugh. I like watching television. That is how I know about the Indians."

"That was the Indians many years ago. Today we are just like you. We live in houses, hold jobs, marry and have children. We go to school and mind our parents." Richard showed Jeremiah his badge and ID. "I had to go to college and make good grades to do what I do. I have put little boys like you in jail many times because they were in places they had no business being. I also arrested the men that let them in those places and they are still in jail. Did you ever think you would go to jail because you **are** breaking the law?"

Jacob had quietly come in and heard Richard's statement. He sat down near Charity.

Jeremiah looked at Richard with a sneer. "No I am not going to jail and it is none of your business."

Joseph jumped up. "Charity, I told you he was going to get out of hand and be in trouble."

Jacob reached and grabbed Jeremiah on his lap. "Grandson, we do not hit and fight as Amish, but we sure spank our children when they need it." With that he turned Jeremiah over his knee, and with his open hand, gave him several whacks on his bottom.

Charity was shocked. She put her hand over her mouth with tears streaming down her cheeks. Finally she was able to speak. "Jeremiah, go to your room and stay there until I can come talk to you." He didn't cry; just stomped out of the room and ran up the stairs, slamming his bedroom door.

Jacob put his arm around Charity. "That is the trouble. You have just talked to him. He is strong-headed like you and also has some of Adam's willfulness. He needs a man around the house. You have been a widow almost ten years now. It is past time you find a husband."

"But daed," she cried, "I do not want another husband. I still love Adam and my heart can not hold more."

"We will talk about this another time. I assume you are the man who saved my daughter today." Jacob reached to shake hands with Richard.

"Yes, sir," Richard stood up. "Well, I don't know how much saving I did, but everything turned out all right. Thank God for that."

"Ja. Danki Gott. I must apologize for having a family problem in front of you. As the Grandfather I feel it is my place to set the standards. Jeremiah is too young to be baptized and join the church, but he needs to know how to conduct himself as a Christian Amish. I love my daughter, maybe too much, but she has been too easy on him, and he takes advantage of her."

Jacob turned to Charity. "You listen good, young lady. You tell him he is not to go anywhere, or do anything, with this Monroe boy. If he goes in the sports bar again, I will give him a really good spanking and then take Sheriff Fleming in to have a serious talk with the owner. In fact, I think I will talk to him anyway."

Charity looked at her daed, whom she loved dearly, and with tear-filled eyes answered, "He is still my son. You did a wonderful job of raising us, but Jeremiah is my responsibility."

Joseph came to stand by Charity. She was surprised at how tall he had grown. He was her little brother and she had thought of him that way. She suddenly realized that he was a grown man and taller than she was. "You are my big sister and I love you dearly, but I know how some of the other boys have gone off, down the wrong path, and broke their families' hearts. Jeremiah is very headstrong and unless he is taught properly, he will break your heart even before he is old enough for rumspringa."

"Danki, Joseph. I know you love me and Jeremiah, and I know you mean well, but please don't undermine my relationship with my son. I promise that I will talk seriously to him and from now on, he will give up something he really counts on if he gets out of line. Yes, he needs to learn self-discipline and responsibility."

"Richard," Jacob addressed him, "are you staying the night? You will be welcome at my house."

"Thank you, sir, but I will stay here with Charity. It looks as if she needs a friend."

"Daed, please ask Alicia to come stay the night. She will be enough chaperone. Would you both like to stay for supper?"

"No, thank you. We will go on home. I do love you dearly and love Jeremiah. Your mother would be heartbroken if she could see how smart mouthed and willful he has become."

"You are blaming me for that?"

"Who else has been responsible for him? We have helped you all we can, taking care of him when you were at work and having him work with us."

Joseph hugged her to show he still loved her.

Jacob quoted, "He who spares the rod hates his son, but he who loves him is careful to discipline him." (Proverbs 13:24) "Train a child in the way he should go, and when he is old he will not turn from it." (Proverbs 22:6)

Joseph, like Charity, had started through rumspringa and decided it was not for him. He had been baptized and was a church member. He was not ready to get married and settle down, but he was preparing for it. Like Charity, he was concerned about Alicia. She was such an innocent and had not had the experience of doing much on her own. None of them worried about Maeve. She was like their mother, a hard worker, gentle and easy-going. Alicia was older than the usual Amish girl for rumspringa.

Jacob and Joseph left with the promise to send Alicia over. Charity fixed ham, fried potatoes, green beans, salad, heated yeast rolls, and made coffee.

She poured milk for Jeremiah and called him to supper.

"I do not want to eat."

"It is supper time. Please come to the table and be part of the family."

"Am I really part of the family? Everyone thinks I am so bad and no one likes me any more."

"Jeremih, you know that is not true. You did not act like a true Amish and your Grossfadder spanked you; only because he loves you and wants you to be responsible for your actions. Come on to the table. I do not want to hear any more of this."

"You did not hear me. I AM NOT COMING TO SUPPER."

"You are going to get mighty hungry before breakfast."

There was silence, so Charity, very sad, apologized to Richard and sat down to eat with him. She was surprised when he bowed his head and prayed aloud. She must have looked surprised for when he raised his head and looked at her, he gave a puzzled smile.

"Don't you pray before meals?"

"Ja. Before and after, but we do not speak out loud. We go by the verse in Matthew 6:6 *When you pray, go into your room, close the door and pray. Do not keep on babbling like pagans, for they think they will be heard because of their many words. Your Father knows what you need before you ask.* And then we have Deuteronomy 8: 10 *When you have eaten and are satisfied, praise the Lord your God.* We feel that pray is of the heart between you and God and no one else needs to hear."

"Oh. I didn't know that. We do pray aloud. Should I apologize?"

"Nee! No. It is fine. You do what you have been trained to do. I am pleased that you believe in God and in prayer."

"Charity, I couldn't have lived through some of my work if I hadn't prayed for help and guidance."

"Gut. Here, eat yourself full." He laughed in astonishment.

"That I'll do. Everything looks good and smells so good. Thank you for allowing me to have a home-cooked meal and a place to stay. I'll be out of your way tomorrow." He looked solemn. "I wish I was here long enough to work with Jeremiah. Your father is right. Nothing against you, but he is a headstrong boy who needs a man in the house."

"He has been so good up until now."

"He is older, observing more of the world around him, and being influenced by boys in school and town. Let your father and brothers help. They love both of you and want him to become a good man."

"I know," she said bowing her head. "They love us and mean well. It just feels as if they think I am not a good mother."

"I'm sure you're a wonderful mother. Some children just need a stronger hand when they have such an independent spirit."

"Ja. I know what you are saying and I know it is the truth. It is just that I have missed my husband so much and have been too easy on my son to make up for him not having a father."

"I can understand that, but it hasn't been good for Jeremiah. Now where do you want me to sleep? I don't need to butt into your business."

"I will show you the guest room, and do not feel you are butting in. You are a welcome guest. I want you to feel free to stay with us in the future, if you come this way again. Oh, here is my sister, Alicia, who will stay with me tonight. Alicia, this is Richard Longbow and I know you have heard the news of the day by now."

"Ja. I have, and right worried I have been. Do you think it is safe to have a store in town?"

"There is nothing wrong with having a store in town. Those bad men just happened to find our town by accident, or so they said. I doubt that I will ever have any more trouble. Have you eaten?"

"Ja. Danki. I will wash the dishes and clean the kitchen. Then we will go to bed and talk there. Mr. Longbow, it is nice to meet you."

Richard went up to bed quietly and thankfully. He read the Bible that he carried with him and prayed for Charity and Jeremiah. He thanked God for allowing him to capture the criminal with no shooting or bloodshed.

In her room, Charity was crying and asking God to direct her how to deal with Jeremiah. Why was he so angry? What had happened to her happy, smiling boy? Should she really be thinking of marrying again so that a man could guide Jeremiah? No, she had men folks in her family who were all willing to help with him.

Alicia came up to bed and hung her dress on a peg on the wall. She placed her shoes neatly on the floor on her side of the bed and put on a gown that Charity had made. She said her prayer and then turned to Charity. They talked quietly for a few minutes and then both women drifted off to sleep to awaken at five the next morning.

CHAPTER THIRTEEN

Jeremiah came down sullen and scowling. He did not speak to either Richard or his mother. He went out silently and did his chores and then came in to wash his hands and sit at the table.

Richard asked a blessing with Jeremiah staring wide-eyed at him. Charity leaned over to kiss Jeremiah's cheek, but he ducked from her. With tearful eyes she tried to smile. Alicia smiled at her in encouragement.

"Good morning my son. I hope you had a good night and are ready for a wonderful day. I will be anxious to hear what you will study today in school." Jeremiah still said nothing. Richard tried to talk to him but he only glared at Richard and would not say a word.

While they were eating oatmeal, scrambled eggs, pancakes, apple butter, coffee or milk, a car was heard in the driveway. Charity got up to see who could be coming at that hour of the morning driving a car. She was pleasantly surprised to welcome Dr. Yoder. She introduced him to Richard and invited him to sit and have breakfast with them.

Charity told Richard of her trip to Shipshewanna and the men who attacked her. She explained that Dr. Yoder was the physician who took care of her in the hospital there and why he was now here in Shickshinny.

Jeremiah, still not speaking, stomped up to brush his teeth and get his material for school for the day. He went out the back door without speaking and got in the carriage with Marilyn.

Isaac Yoder noticed Jeremiah's behavior, but wisely said nothing. He and Richard exchanged a knowing look. "Forgive me for just dropping in, Charity. I heard about the trouble in town and came to see for myself how you are getting along. Where in the world is your guardian angel? Too much unpleasantness is happing to you." He smiled.

"Would you like some breakfast? It would be no trouble at all."

"No, thank you. I've eaten and need to cut back anyway. I'm getting too portly around the middle," he laughed.

They talked a few minutes then Richard took his cell phone and called his partner, Derek Echohawk. Derek promised to fly out ASAP and help Richard escort the prisoners back to the west where they were wanted for multi crimes.

Richard stood and smiled. "Thank you, Charity, for your delicious food, the feather bed on which I was so comfortable and for allowing me to be part of your family for a short time. I must get to town and talk to the sheriff about our prisoners." He turned to Isaac. "It's a pleasure to meet you and know Charity has a wonderful friend near. Take good care of her and that troubled son of hers."

"Charity," Isaac said, "I'm going to give Richard a ride to town. May I come back later today and talk to you about something very important?"

"Ja. You are welcome any time. I will be home today for Rosemary and the girls will handle the store."

Richard and Isaac left. As Charity was cleaning the kitchen she prayed for Jeremiah and for her to be a better mother. "Got, please show me the way to help my son. He truly is troubled and I do not know what to do about it."

Isaac was kept with an emergency at the hospital and was not able to get back to Charity until the evening. He felt it was too late to bother her, besides, he wanted to talk to her when Jeremiah was in school.

Charity was glad to see Jeremiah coming home from school. She determined to not question him or cause any unpleasantness today. She had one of his favorite snacks ready for dinner would be a little late. Jacob, Joshua, Michael and Lawrence were coming over to try to talk to Jeremiah.

Jeremiah didn't even thank her, as he usually did, for the snack, a Popeye.

This was a thick slice of bread with a hole pulled in the middle. An egg was broken into this hole and the whole thing was fried in hot butter. She had no idea where he had heard of the food, but thought it must have come from one of his English friends. She did so wish he would talk and tell her what was bothering him.

He at his Popeye and drank a mug of hot chocolate. He sat at the kitchen table and started his homework while his mother prepared supper. She had fixed chicken and dumplings, green beans, hot apple slices, hominy and coffee or cider. Milk for Jeremiah and sometimes Lawrence,

Jeremiah had just finished his school work when his grandfather and uncles came in. He didn't run to greet them as he used to do. He didn't even acknowledge them and had been silent with his mother. They looked at each other, but said nothing. They all sat down and had their silent prayer.

Jacob looked up and noticed that Jeremiah had not bowed his head, but was instead looking around. He was upset, but still said nothing.

They talked with Charity about her store and the news of the town. When one of them would speak to Jeremiah, he would just glare at them and shrug his shoulder.

When everyone had finished and still sat at the table with a cup of coffee, Charity got up and washed the dishes quickly and wiped the counter off. She sat at the table with a cup of coffee.

Jacob clear his throat, "Grandson, I have come to talk to you." Jeremiah just stared at his with his upper lip curled in one corner. "The whole church is praying for you. We are all disturbed because you have not been the kind, mannerly young man that you have been trained to be." Jeremiah still didn't say anything, just looked at Jacob. "We love you and want to help. Can you tell me why you are so unhappy?"

Jeremiah said nothing. He stood so quickly that his chair fell over and glaring at his grandfather walked out of the room and went upstairs.

Charity was crying so hard that her dad got up and came around to hold her on his lap and hug as he did when she was little. Michael and Lawrence both looked as if they would like to cry. They were all heartsick.

After praying with Charity, the men decided to leave and allow Charity to try to calm down.

Lawrence came running back in. "Charity, I know it is not the Amish way, but maybe it would help to take him to a child psychiatrist."

She was so hurt and now shocked that she didn't know what to say. "I would like to talk to Isaac Yoder and see what he can recommend. I am not against the help of a psychiatrist if it will do any good for Jeremiah." He hugged her again and left.

Weeks went by with no change in Jeremiah's attitude. Everyone noticed that Charity was losing weight and had dark circles under her eyes. Her family and friends became afraid for her health.

One day, after work, Michael rushed into Charity's house. He noticed Jeremiah pausing before he went upstairs. "Charity, please put on a coat and come outside." Puzzled she got her coat and bonnet and followed him outside. They walked over to the fence away from the house. Michael looked up and saw Jeremiah watching them from a window.

"What did you want , Michael? Why all the secrecy"?

"I did not want Jeremiah to over hear what I am going to tell you. Deputy Glenn Harrison saw me in town today and gave me some distressing news. He saw a group of teenagers, English, standing on a corner and smoking. They were laughing and talking loudly and acting as if they were on drugs. He was shocked to see Jeremiah with them and he, too, was smoking."

Charity's hand flew to her mouth to cover a sound she did not want to make. "Is he sure? It was my Jeremiah?"

"Oh, yes. Everyone in town knows Jeremiah. Several people have told me they do not like the looks of the boys he is associating with. We will have to be calm about this and decide the best plan to take. I will talk to daed and Joshua and we will get back with you." He hugged her and left. She stayed out a little longer not realizing that Jeremiah was watching her.

It was very hard for Charity to go back in the house and be calm. She wanted to call Jeremiah down and question him, but she knew it would just make things worse. She was startled to see him standing in the kitchen glaring at her as she came in the door. She tried to smile. "Are you as hungry as I am? If you will give me a little time I will heat something or we can have cornbread and milk with the banana cream pie I made today."

"I'm not hungry," he snarled and stamped up the stairs and slammed the door to his room. She was so upset, she did not notice he answered her as an English boy would and not as an Amish.

She sat for a long time reading her Bible and praying. Finally she went up to bed without eating.

CHAPTER FOURTEEN

Jacob made a special trip to town and talked to Micah. Yes, Micah had been told about seeing the boys with Jeremiah. "Jacob, do you want me to talk to Jeremiah? I will if you think it will be of any benefit. At this time I'm not sure what is the best approach."

"Nee. No. Thank you. None of us know what is best. We are all shocked and heartsick. Not a one of my children ever gave me trouble like this. I can not imagine why Jeremiah is giving us so much trouble. He will not talk to us or answer any of our questions. Charity is so worried her health is failing. I am at my wit's end. Pray with us and let us hope we find the answer before it is too late."

Micah knelt at Jacob's knees and prayed aloud. Jacob kept his head bowed and his eyes shut. He was not accustomed to hearing prayers aloud. When he opened his eyes, he was surprised to see three deputies on their knees with their hands on Micah's shoulders giving him spiritual support.

He was very grateful and choked when he tried to thank them. They all slapped him on the back and shook his hand stating that they would keep an eye out for Jeremiah and keep on praying.

Jacob went home a little more comforted but still not sure what to do. He stopped at the store to tell Charity what he had done and how the men had responded. She was touched and grateful. She tearfully told him she had word that Jeremiah was skipping school.

"Charity, I am going to call a family conference, including the Kimes, after all he is their grandson, also. We must get to the bottom of this before something terrible happens and it I too late."

"I know, daed. I appreciate all that all of you have done. I do not know where to turn now. I am almost ready to follow Lawrence's suggestion and take Jeremiah to a psychiatrist."

"Give us time to all talk one more time. I am not against him talking to a psychiatrist if it will help. I can pay for it if you want to go that way."

"Thank the good Lord I can pay for it myself. My store is doing well enough so that I can afford things I could not before."

It was not a secret because the church had been praying for Jeremiah and the whole town was now aware of the problem. Still Charity hated to talk about it to her workers and volunteers. Rosemary reminded her that they were all friends and loved her dearly. They were all interested in doing what they could.

With a heavy heart she worked through the day and left feeling as if she were carrying the weight of the world. At home Jeremiah still would not talk to her even when she called him to her.

"Jeremiah, I am very distressed to hear that you are skipping school and associating with a rough crowd of boys. Is this true?"

He shrugged his shoulders, pushed past her and went out to do his chores. She was thankful he was doing that much. She began to get a supper for them. Jeremiah came in, washed, sat down at the table, but would not bow his head for silent prayers.

"My darling son, I love you so much. Your daed and grosmudder love you from Heaven. Why have you turned away from praying?"

"Miles Jordan asks me questions about what we do. He said it all sounded very silly and hard to follow. And it is. How do we really know there is a God and how do we know He cares what happens to us?"

"Oh, my. That's where faith comes in. How can you question God when we have so many blessings?"

"He took my daed and grosmudder Jenna. He did not love us enough to leave them with us."

"No! God did not take them to punish us. Your daed was killed by a very bad man who was led by the devil and your grosmudder was very sick. She had a bad disease that had eaten her lungs and kept her from breathing. God took her to Heaven to heal her and your daed is very happy with God."

"How do you know?"

"I believe what the Biewel tells us. You need to read it more. Now, please, finish your school work."

"But, mamm, if God is so good, why did He let the men hurt you and put you in the hospital?"

"He did not let them and He took care of me by sending the men to fight the bad men. The bad men were just doing what the devil told them to do. And I hear that the boys you are friendly with are being led by the devil."

"But, mamm, we are not calling the devil to lead us."

"The devil does not wait to be called. He is always ready to step in and make matters worse. He does not care if he breaks hearts or causes people to lose their life."

Charity did not care what they were talking about as long as her son was open with her. She was so relieved that he at last was talking. "Will you think about this, Jeremiah, and come to me whenever you are confused or need to talk?"

Jeremiah apparently thought of what he was doing. He jerked his shoulder and started out of the room. "I have friends I can trust and they care about me." He ran up the stairs and slammed his bedroom door.

Charity was again hurting in her heart and not knowing what else to do. She thought of mamm Leah saying, "*But those who hope in the Lord will renew their strength. They will soar on wings like eagles; they will run and not grow weary; they will walk and not be faint.*" (Isaiah 40:31) She remembered her mother saying, "*We also rejoice in our sufferings because we know that suffering produces perseverance, character, and hope. And hope does not disappoint us because God has poured out His divine love into our hearts by the Holy Spirit whom He has given us.*" (Romans 5:3)

Charity was holding her arms across her chest and rocking back and forth in the straight chair in the kitchen when the door opened. With sorrowful eyes she looked to see Jacob, Joshua, Leah, Michael, Deborah, Alicia, Maeve, Joseph, Belinda, Marysue and Lawrence.

Adam had made a long table expecting to have several children and guests. Charity had the men bring in chairs from the front room and they all sat around the kitchen table with a thirty cup pot of coffee in front of them.

Sugar, cream and pastries were on the table with ironed cloth napkins. They had each just poured a cup of coffee when Sheriff Micah Fleming came in.

"Brrr. It's cold out there," he shivered.

"Better out than in here," Joshua spoke dryly.

"Micah, would you like some coffee?" Charity welcomed him.

"Yes, please, and those apple dumplings look mighty good. Did you make them, Charity?"

"Ja, and they are still warm. Would you like fresh, thick cream on one?"

"No, thank you. Just the dumpling. Now will someone tell me why I was invited to this gathering?"

Jacob cleared his throat. "I invited you because we have talked some of this problem before. We are all very concerned about Jeremiah. He has changed so much from a well-mannered, loving boy to a smart-mouthed ruffian who is associating with a rough crowd of older boys. We need to help him and make him know that we love him and want to help him."

Charity told them of the conversation she had with Jeremiah before he went to bed. "He is hurting because he is listening to boys who are not God fearing and have no respect for themselves or others. I would like to know what kind of homes they are from."

There was a murmur of assent, but no one spoke. Finally Lawrence said, "Micah, I suggested a child psychiatrist. I do not know that it would do any good, but at least we would be trying something. We have all talked to him and you heard how he talked to his mother tonight."

"Yes, and you don't know how sorry I am. I know and respected Adam, and I know, for a fact, that Charity has been an excellent mother."

"She has not been strict enough," Joshua spoke slowly. "He needs a man for a role model and a firm hand. We have done what we could, but it is not like being with him all of the time."

Leah was almost sobbing. She wiped the tears from her cheek. "I can understand why Charity has not found it necessary to get married. She did love my son with her whole heart and no other man has been able to fill that place with her. I do not think his behavior is because he does not have a man living with them. I think it is all those hoodlums he is seeing and listening to them talk nonsense."

"He is almost ten years old and already big for his age. There is no question that he is intelligent and capable of becoming someone great. I wish I knew how to help him save himself." Michael wiped his own eyes.

Micah stood. "Let's all keep praying about this and I'll get the teens together and talk to them. I might have to go to some of the homes because I doubt that all the parents are aware of their sons' bad habits. Those teens need to be in school, also."

They thanked Micah for coming because he had to get home to his family. They just sat sadly looking at each other.

Jacob stood. "Well, if no one has anything else to say, I am going to go with Lawrence's suggestion for a child psychiatrist. Everyone go home and keep praying."

"Thank you for your caring and your support. I do not know what I would do without all of you. I love you all. I love my precious son so much and my heart breaks for him. Yes, we will try the psychiatrist. I know it will not change overnight, but I can pray and hope."

Charity tossed and turned unable to relax and sleep. The morning came far too soon and she got up to go out and do the chores. She dressed warmly for it was very cold. Going through the kitchen she decided to start a pot of coffee so that it would be ready when she came back in. Setting cream and sugar out on the table and laying plates and tableware, she saw a sheet of paper with writing on it. Puzzled she picked it up, read through it twice and sat down heavily because her legs were folding beneath her.

The paper read:

Mamm, I heard all of you talking about me tonight. I do not want to go to a sikiatrist or to anyone. I am going with the boys who do like me and want me to be with them. They said we are like a family together. I hope you will stay well. Get Joseph to help you with the chores.

Jerry

She ran up to his bedroom. Empty. His backpack was gone but his school books were on a table. He must have put some clothes in the backpack.

She ran back down to the kitchen. Her canvas bag was missing and so was some of the food.

She fell to the floor and did not stir when the door opened.

CHAPTER FIFTEEN

"Charity, I am here to help you with your chores. I have already fed the horses and milked the cow. I need something hot before I --- Charity!"

Joseph raced across the floor to his sister. "Charity. Please wake up. Charity, are you all right?" He was lightly smacking her cold cheeks.

She moaned but didn't stir. He began to be afraid for her. He was just on the verge of calling for Jeremiah to go get Jacob when he saw the paper that had fallen from her hand. He read the note and then snorted. "He has done it again. His answer to everything is to run away."

I can not go off and leave Charity, but I must get daed and start the search for that bothersome boy. His thoughts were running too fast to think of everything. She had lost so much weight that he easily picked her up and carried her to the sofa. Carefully placing her on the sofa, he began to rub her cold hands and call her name. She would only moan and move her head from side to side.

Joseph could only pray. He spoke aloud in the traditional Amish language. "O Gott Vater (Oh loving Father) please be with my sister. Warm her with your love and keep her safe. Help us to find that disobedient boy and bring him home to her. He is all she has now besides our own family."

He was praying so loudly that he did not hear Alicia come in. She nearly made him pass out when she shrieked in his ear and said, in a frightened voice, "Why is Charity so still? What is wrong? Where is Jeremiah?" He couldn't talk at the moment; he just handed her the note.

"Oh, that little devil. I will stay with sister. You run get daed and we will decide what to do." Alicia took charge by covering Charity with more blankets and rubbing her wrists.

Joseph ran so fast he forgot to put on his coat, gloves or hat. It alarmed Jacob when Joseph ran into the barn where he was working. His son was red in the face, shaking, trying to keep from crying and out in the cold with little clothing on.

Jacob put his arms round Joseph, surprised that they were the same height. He tried to warm Joseph and get him to tell why he was in such a state.

Finally Joseph got control of his emotions enough to tell his daed about Charity and the note. "Alicia is with her, but she has had an awful shock."

"Go to our English neighbors near here and call Micah, then call Isaac Yoder." Joseph dashed away still with no outer clothing in the bitter cold air.

Just as Jacob was getting ready to leave, Michael came by on his way to town. Jacob was so glad to see him. "Tell the girls at the store that they will have to take over for a while. I do not know what the future holds for us. I feel like taking a belt to Jeremiah, but I know that is not the right thing to do."

Micah pulled into Jacob's driveway as he told Maeve where he would be and was preparing to leave. Micah took him in the car across to Charity's.

Jacob could only tell him what Joseph had said.

The first thing Micah did was to check on Charity. She was still out and Alicia was frantic. He then wanted to read the note and take it for his records.

It wasn't long until Dr. Yoder pulled in. He ran into the house. "What's this I hear about Charity collapsing and Jeremiah running away?" He was told the happenings of the day and shown the note from Jeremiah. He just shook his head and grumbled under his breath.

Checking Charity he decided that nature had found a way to take care of Charity. "There's no way I can tell how long she'll be unconscious or what condition she will be in. I'm going to take her to the hospital and give her fluids through IVs. She will need to be monitored until she is strong enough to face what is happening. She has worried over Jeremiah and her place of business until she is so run down that she's in a dangerous stage."

Jacob trusted Dr. Yoder and allowed him to go to his car and call for an ambulance. He asked him to call the English neighbor and please tell them to contact Joshua for him. Jacob and Joshua had been together all their lives and felt as brothers to each other. Besides, Joshua was still Charity's father-in-law.

Joshua asked the English neighbor to drive him to the hospital and meet Jacob there. They stayed together, giving comfort to each other, until Charity was placed in a private room. The two men stayed with her after asking an Amish nurse to contact the Bishop for them. They waited for the Bishop to come so they could pray together. Of course both men were already praying in their own minds and hearts.

In the meantime Micah had gone to the high school and found the names of the boys and their addresses. Going to the homes he discovered that four of the five boys were also missing. One of the families was very distressed and even more so when they heard that their son had been instrumental in teaching a young boy to be temperamental and of bad behavior.

The fifth boy had backed out of going with them. His father ordered him to sit down with Micah and tell what had been going on. He told of breaking and entering homes and stealing. He told that some of the boys had stolen their fathers' credit cards and had gotten money on them. They were prepared to leave. James Morton told them he had not felt right in encouraging Jeremiah to smoke or to steal. The boys wanted him with them because he was smaller and could get in places that were difficult for them. Too, if they were caught, they could blame everything on Jeremiah and because he was so young, the law would do little to him. They had all progressed to smoking drugs.

Micah informed James that they could all go to Juvenile Hall and Jeremiah would be taken away from his mother and placed in a foster home somewhere. James was horrified at what they had done and finally told that they had planned to go south where it is warmer.

Joseph went back to Charity's shaking from the cold. Alicia made him sit and warm up with hot chocolate before he went out again. He put on his outer clothes and went out to feed the chickens and hogs and gather the eggs. He and Alicia wished they had a phone so they could call the hospital and be kept informed about their sister.

Alicia and Joseph stayed at Charity's until late afternoon when Jacob and Joshua came in with Micah. News was exchanged, but no one felt comforted. Alicia said she would stay at Charity's in case she was brought home. Joseph asked his daed if he could stay and do the chores. Brother and sister could only grieve and wait. Alicia made supper for them. Joseph got Adam's big family Bible and read passages from it. They had prayer and each went on to bed. Jacob and Joshua had gone home after supper.

Everyone spent a fretful night, worrying about Charity and Jeremiah. Jacob was afraid this trouble might affect Charity's mind. He was very upset to hear what the boys had been doing and how they planned to use Jeremiah.

Two days later, Charity had still not awakened. It was a Sunday for the worship service which was to be held with Joshua and Leah. Michael and Lawrence, with other men, had gone to help set the house for service. Alicia, Maeve, Belinda and Marysue took charge of preparing food because Leah did not feel well.

Joshua understood that Jacob wanted to be at the hospital as much as he could and make excuses for him for not attending. There was strong concentrated prayer for Charity and Jeremiah. Bishop Yoder suggested that they pray for all the boys involved that they would come to their senses and grow to be useful citizens.

No one could understand why Jeremiah had gotten into so much trouble and especially of this kind. Dr. Yoder explained that Jeremiah had most of the time been treated as another adult. He was basking in the attention of the teen boys because Jeremiah was intelligent and bored with regular school work.

The day before, when the men had set up the benches, they had placed the Ausbund on the benches for use during the service. The Ausbund contains old songs originating with the Anabaptist captives held at the Oberhaus castle prison in 1535 to 1540 which is in present day southeastern Germany. There are no music notes, just the words. It was first printed in 1564 and is still in use which makes it the oldest song book still in continuous use.

Most of the songs are of the suffering and faith of those in prison who made up verses to express themselves. Other songs have been added through the years. The singing will last thirty minutes, or more, at the beginning of the service. One is usually sung at the closing.

Song practices are held during the week where mostly men attend. The song leader has learned the songs in other communities. He sings one line at a time with the people repeating after him until they memorize the songs.

Benuel Blank, who researched the songs, said they were for the soul rather than the ear. The songs include THE LORD'S PRAYER, OLD TESTAMENT PSALMS and others. I was surprised to learn they had "In The Sweet By and By just as we do. Various church groups have changed some of the songs to fill their needs. One of the best known is Das Loblied (Hymn of Praise). It is sung in every gathering. Mr. Blank says, "Let us thank God for our heritage of song. Though voices have been silenced by martyrs' deaths, congregational singing is an important part of Amish worship." (See Das Loblied at the end of the book.)

Micah had sent word through the law enforcement messages to BOLO, be on the look out, for the teens and a younger boy with them. The people gathered in homes several times during the week to add times of prayer. Jacob sat by Charity's bed and held her hand until everyone began to fear for his health. He was seventy and had worked hard all of his life. He was not eating properly and certainly not resting.

On Tuesday Charity began to stir. She blinked her eyes and seemed surprised to see her daed holding her hand. He leaned over and kissed her forehead and spoke lovingly to her.

"Hello daed. Where am I?"

"You are in the hospital and I am going to call Dr. Yoder right now. He has been so concerned about you and the nurses have been caring well for you."

"Why am I here, daed and how long have I been here?"

"You have been here five days and - - here's Dr. Yoder. He can tell you why you are here."

"Well, welcome back, Sleeping Beauty. You've had us worried. How do you feel now?"

"Fine, but why am I here?"

"First, you must eat something. How about some oatmeal or grits, either one with lots of butter? Just soft foods first that you can swallow without choking. Jello, ice cream, what would you like?"

"Why are you not telling me why I am here?"

"Charity, I want to be sure you are strong enough to discuss it with us."

"Oh, now I remember," she sobbed. "Have you found Jeremiah?"

Jacob took her hand again. "No, daughter, but we know the boys he left with and where they might be going. Micah has law enforcement in several states on the alert for them."

"Where are they going? Who are the boys?"

"You do not know any of the boys. Micah has talked to their families and found that they were not fully aware of the circumstances. One family did not seem to care and that, apparently, is the ring leader."

"But why did they want to leave? What have they done and has Jeremiah done as they have?"

Micah walked into the room with his wife, Anita. She came over to kiss Charity on the cheek and offer her shoulder at any time for tears, conversation or just comforting. Charity could not keep from crying. She missed her sweet mother and here was a woman offering to mother her with caring and love.

"Micah, please tell me what you have found out." Charity begged.

Micah looked at Dr. Yoder who shrugged and nodded.

"Well, I was upset to find that they were not only smoking cigarettes, but were also smoking drugs and drinking. They have been breaking and entering, stealing items including money and running up bills on their parents. One boy who stayed behind told me that they used Jeremiah to get into places that they were too big to fit. Too, if the police ever caught them, they were going to let Jeremiah take the blame thinking he would get off because he is younger. I reminded the boy that Jeremiah could be taken from you and placed in a foster home or a Juvenile home."

"Oh, Micah. You will not take him away from me, will you?"

"It isn't up to me, Charity. The judge will make that decision."

They talked a few more minutes and then Isaac Yoder told all of them they would have to leave. He didn't want Charity getting too tired or over excited. Jacob kissed her cheek and reluctantly left with Micah.

After Charity ate a few bites, and used the restroom, Isaac ordered a relaxant placed in her IV so she would sleep and recuperate.

Chapter Sixteen

Jeremiah was losing the thrill of being with older boys who paid him a lot of attention. He had never felt so grubby in his life. He had lived and slept in his clothes since leaving home. They had eaten all he had brought and were now stealing to eat. They stole clean clothes off clothes lines and committed acts of vandalism for the fun of it.

Morton Richardson (Morty) was seventeen and the ring leader. Thomas Garrison and Benjamin Hamilton were both sixteen. Tracy Goodson would be sixteen the next month. Morty had been the most vocal in laughing and making fun of the Amish ways. He made Jeremiah feel very big and important when he slapped him on the shoulder and told him he was too good for that kind of life.

Jeremiah was very uncomfortable. They were outside of Fayetteville, North Carolina hiding in a rural area. Morty had pushed Jeremiah in the Haw River while laughing and saying he was baptizing him out of the Amish faith. His conscience was beginning to bother him. He thought of how hard his mother worked and how loving she was. When Morty teased him, he felt anger toward his mother for treating him like a baby.

What is wrong with me? Why can I not enjoy being with these boys as I first did. Why do I feel so guilty when we steal something and cause trouble for someone? Morty even took a knife and cut a man's tires and broke a window on his car when he ordered us off his lawn. I felt very bad for the man. He reminded me of grossvater with his white hair and long white beard. He was not Amish, but he could pass for one.

"Hey, knucklehead," Morty pushed Jeremiah. "What are you thinking looking so serious and shaking your head?"

"You want to know the truth? I am thinking I am tired, hungry, very dirty and feeling badly that I have caused grief for my mother."

"Aw don't be such a sissy. We can do without parents. They are a big headache and have too many rules that are crazy. We can take care of ourselves. We need to be free. With us you don't have to do all that work. Best of all you don't have to go to school."

"But I like school and the work. I love the animals and love tending to them. The milk from our cow is the best and we have the best eggs that mamm makes into delicious pancakes and other things."

"Listen to the baby. Mamm. Why don't you say mom or old lady or old bag like I do?"

"Mamm is mom and she is not an old lady. She is beautiful and everyone loves her. I miss hearing her sing as she works."

"Well, do you want to leave us and go back home, little baby?"

The other three boys looked at each other and dropped their heads. They looked as if they would like to go home, also, but none of them dared to say anything to Morty. He was quick with his fists and feet.

Jeremiah began to think of the strict rules at home and thought he might not be so bad off after all. Yes, this was a different life, but he was free.

The man, whose car had been damaged, had given the police a report. Reading his report on four boys, one of them very young, the police chief remembered the BOLO from Sheriff Micah Fleming. He sent an order to all foot patrolmen, and cars to BOLO for the boys. Take them all, especially the youngest one.

As they walked away from Fayetteville, Thomas was limping. He had sprained his ankle when he fell over some big potted plants at a house they were robbing. They hadn't thought that going through the refrigerator and searching for money or anything they could sell, would leave fingerprints.

They had been gone nine days now on their way to Florida where they were eager to live on the beach and live free. Jeremiah and the three boys were getting tired of Morty bullying them and making all the decisions. They were all too afraid of him to protest.

Jeremiah was thinking all the time. Live free? What about school, clothes, food, shelter and most of all people? He missed all his relatives. But most of all he missed his mother. Besides, he was having headaches that would not go away. Sometimes the aches made him dizzy and his eyesight blurred. He was afraid to let the others know how sick he sometimes felt. He was afraid Morty would follow through with his threat to leave him behind. How could he get along on his own?

Jeremiah was secretly relieved when a North Carolina state police car pulled up and stopped ahead of them. His mouth dropped open. Was that Sheriff Fleming getting out of the car with the officer?

"Jeremiah, I am so glad to see you. I'm glad to see all you boys. There have been a lot of people worried about all of you. Jeremiah, the church has held dozens of prayer meetings for you."

Jeremiah was determined that he would not cry in front of the other boys, although he felt like crying. His head hurt so bad and he was hungry and grubby.

Morty had taking off running when the car had stopped. The officer didn't know whether to run after him or take in the other four boys. He turned to Micah.

"Do you want to take charge of these boys since they are from your town?"

"Yes, thank you," Micah answered. "If your chief will be so kind as to tell me how I can get them cleaned up, fed and housed for the night."

"Oh, the boys will be in a cell. You will go to the hotel as a guest of the city."

"Thank you, Officer Parsons, but couldn't I take the youngest with me? I'm sure he won't run away and he'll be fine with me."

"Let's take them back to the office and ask the chief what he wants to do."

Micah had been thinking as they took the boys to the jail. He took Officer Parsons off to one side as they got out of the car. "I've been thinking, and I've changed my mind. Leaving Jeremiah in jail for the night might be a good lesson."

"I agree, but let's talk to the chief. Come on, boys. Let's get you cleaned up and fed. A good night's rest will be good for you before you head back home."

Chief Bernard Donaldson agreed that it would be best for the boys to spend a night in cells. "Fortunately, we only have one cell occupied. I'll keep the boys at the far end away from the two drunks who were fighting."

Micah walked to where the boys were seated with an officer guarding them. "Jeremiah, I'm sorry, but you have to stay in jail for the night."

Jeremiah did break down and start to cry. The other boys put their arms around him and tried to comfort him.

"Just think," Tracy calmed him. "We'll be home with out folks and have a good life. I'm so sorry that I ever listened to Morty. I am sorry that I was one of the crowd and took you away from a good home and a loving mother."

Before anyone could catch him Jeremiah passed out and dropped to the floor. Officer Parsons went with Micah to take him a half mile to a hospital.

Micah asked permission to stay in the room with Jeremiah for the night.

Officer Parsons had asked Micah to call him by his given name. "Leigh, if you'll be so kind, I need to make some long distance calls and tell the families that their wayward children will be coming home."

"May I suggest you wait until the morning and see if you'll be leaving tomorrow. This boy might not be able to travel and we need to get information from the other boys."

"Maybe you're right. Yes, I'll wait, but I know if it were my child I would be very anxious to know he had been found and was all right. What will you do about Morton Richardson who ran? He must be found. I wasn't impressed with his parents and home. His father is a drunk and his mother is a very meek, mild woman. I suspect he is abusive to her and probably beat Morton until he could not take it any more. I hope it isn't too late to rehabilitate him. He needs a lot of love and caring."

"I'm sorry to hear about his home life. Sadly there are too many like that. All of us do the best we can to make the youth know that we do care. Also, to tell the truth, there may be police officers that are not the best example to youngsters like Morton."

Dr. Cooley examined Jeremiah and then turned to Micah and Leigh. "I think he's just dehydrated and probably scared. He looks too young to be so far away from home on his own. What gets into these children?"

"This one just listened to the wrong peer pressure. He is from a good, Bible crowd. He's Amish." Micah explained.

"My goodness. I've heard how God-fearing they are. I'm surprised that a child, raised in that atmosphere, would do something like this."

"I am, too." Micah looked so solemn. "I would like for him to open up and tell me just what the problem is. He's been like this for about a year; arguing, sassing and doing things no Amish child is allowed to do."

"Well, I am a Christian, but I can't begin to understand the Amish. Nothing against them; I just haven't had the opportunity to know them, although I've heard many good things about them. I understand they're hard workers, honest and trustworthy."

"They're all of that and more. They make excellent neighbors. When can we take Jeremiah?"

"Leave him with me for tonight and it'll give us a chance to put liquids in him and, hopefully, solve a lot of his problems."

"Thank you, Dr. Cooley. I have to make some phone calls, but I'll be back. I want to be with him when he wakes up." Micah shook the doctor's hand and left with Officer Leigh Parsons.

The more Micah and Leigh talked, the more he thought about what should be done. "Leigh, I need to get back and talk to your chief about something."

Chief Donaldson was intrigued with Micah's suggestion. "I'll talk to Judge Pearl Stallard and see if she will help us out."

Later that night Jeremiah awakened and was thirsty. He was very concerned about what would be in his future. "Where are Tom, Benny and Tracy?" was his first thought."

"Still in jail," Micah informed him.

"Oh. Will I have to go back to jail?"

"You'll stay here tonight, but tomorrow all of you will have to appear before a judge and follow the directions of the court." Micah couldn't keep from smiling.

Judge Stallard had agreed to the suggestion. Even though it wasn't according to law, Micah wanted to give the boys, especially Jeremiah, a taste of what could happen to them. She would meet them in court tomorrow morning and talk to the boys.

Micah had purchased clean clothes and shoes for Jeremiah. The hospital had furnished toothbrush, toothpaste and a comb. A male nurse helped him shower and dress after his breakfast. Micah took him to the courthouse. Leigh and

Chief Donaldson were there with Thomas, Benjamin and Tracy.

Judge Stallard talked to the three other boys first and scolded them for their behavior. "I've been informed that an older boy led you gentlemen and he was the one who did damage to people's property. He will probably face about five years in jail. As to you three, I think two nights in jail is about right for what you've done. I am going to allow you to go home with Sheriff Fleming and hope you'll remember this and be on your best behavior from now on."

"Yes, your Honor," they answered as they had been instructed to do.

"Will the bailiff bring Jeremiah Adam Kime forward."

Bailiff David Archer put his arm around Jeremiah's shoulder and led him to stand before the bench looking up at the judge. He knew what was being done and tried hard not to smile because he felt Jeremiah shaking.

"Good morning, Jeremiah."

"Goo," choke, "good morning. Your Honor." He was so nervous he could hardly remember his own name.

"Why are you before me, young man?"

"Because I'm stupid, your Honor"

She pounded her gavel when those in court chuckled aloud.

"Why are you stupid? May I call you Jeremiah?"

"You have called me, your Honor," he answered mystified as to why the men behind him keep laughing. He felt like crying.

Judge Stallard cleared her throat and looked at her desk for a moment.

"I want to know why you think you are stupid."

"Because I did not listen to my mamm and grossfader, my mother and grandfather. I didn't follow rules and was not respectful of my mother. I thought I was old enough to be on my own, but I understand that I am not."

He began to sway.

"Jeremiah, do you realize that I have the power to take you away from your mother and grandfather and place you in a Juvenile Home until you are eighteen years old? After thinking it over, and realizing that you are aware of your unfortunate behavior, I am going to let Sheriff Fleming take you home with the provision that you report to him each week for six months until he decides you can be relieved of this order."

"Oh, thank you. Oh, my head sure hurts." He fell to the floor.

Micah thanked the Judge for her cooperation. He shook hands with the chief and his officers and thanked them. Judge Stallard asked to be kept informed as to Jeremiah's condition. She smiled at the other three boys and wished them well hoping that they learned a valuable lesson from this. She then left to enjoy the rest of her day off.

Micah carried Jeremiah out to his car with the three boys following. He placed the boys in the back seat with no inside handles or locks that could be opened from the inside. He then got in the front seat with Benjamin lying down and his head on Micah's lap.

"Is anyone hungry or need to use the bathroom?" They assured him that they didn't. He waved at the officers watching and drove off.

151

He got on Highway 11 and drove north into Virginia. Stopping at a fast food place, just as they approached Richmond, he ordered food and milkshakes for them with apple pies. All four boys went to sleep.

He was later than he wanted to be because they had waited for the court session and to help the boys learn how life could be different. It was up to them.

Micah decided that it would be safer to stop for the night. If he had been alone he would have kept driving and arrived home about midnight. He pulled into a nice looking motel with a restaurant. In the office he explained that he needed a large room with two queen beds and a cot.

"You want your family in the same room with you?" the girl asked.

"Something like that," he smiled.

He was assigned a room on the back side of the motel which suited him fine. He had the boys wash and then took them next door for a supper. They were wide-eyed with the new experience and relieved that they were not in more trouble than they were.

Jeremiah bowed his head for silent prayer, but Micah spoke a short prayer for them. For their safe return, for their families and for their future. The three boys were impressed. They quietly ate and were ready to go back to the motel. They took turns showering and brushing their teeth. Micah gave them clothing that he had purchased for them. This came from a fund he had in his office.

The next morning, they got up washed and dressed in their new clothes, then went next door for breakfast. They were on the road by nine. Micah didn't want to rush because he knew he was tired. Thomas bragged that he could drive and help Micah, but he was reminded that this was a company car which he was not licensed to drive.

"You boys are forgetting that you are technically under arrest until I turn you over to your parents."

"My dad is going to whip the daylights out of me," Tracy shuddered.

"My mother will cry and hug me then slap me good and plenty," Thomas stated.

"Are your parents abusive to you," Micah asked anxiously.

"No," Thomas continued, "my daddy left us when I was six. My mother is holding two jobs to support us and has little time for me. She is a good mother, just very strict. But I understand now why she is so strict."

"My dad makes a good living and provides for us. I have one little brother and one little sister. He's an attorney. He drinks a lot and when he is drinking, he gets mean. He even slaps mom around sometimes, but that only when he's drinking," Benjamin quickly added.

"Same with my dad," Tracy stated. "I know he loves us, but he gambles and when he losses too much he gets nasty. He does drink a beer sometimes, but he's not a drunk."

Jeremiah said nothing, but he listened at what the other boys were saying about their home lives. He was thankful for his mother and understood now why his grandfather had spanked him. He had thought he was too big to be spanked at the time, but now he would gladly be back there.

Micah stopped for a soft drink and to get gas and then thankfully went on the last leg of his journey. He arrived in

Shickshinny around two in the afternoon. He called the parents of the three boys and had then come to the station to claim their son. He wanted to see them and have a serious talk with them. He reminded the boys that he was their friend and would be available if any of them ever needed to talk to him about anything.

CHAPTER SEVENTEEN

Micah saw Lawrence in town and told him to tell Charity and the rest of the family that he was taking Jeremiah to Dr. Yoder. He explained to him about Jeremiah's headaches and passing out. "That isn't natural for a young child. I want him checked out thoroughly. It might explain the change in his personality."

Lawrence went first to the store to tell Charity and all the rest of the workers and volunteers that had been prying for Jeremiah. He saw Deputy Glenn and asked him if he would be so kind as to go tell Jacob and Joshua. He was going to the hospital with Charity.

Isaac Yoder was so relieved to see Jeremiah that he hugged him and scolded him at the same time. "You are very fortunate to have so many people who love you and care about you. We have all been worried sick. Your mother has almost had a breakdown. She loves you so much and feels a deep responsibility to raise you as your father would have done."

"I know and I am honestly sorry. I really did not know how good I have it until I heard the other boys tell about how hard they have it at their homes."

"Well, it's over and done now. Let's put this behind us and do as we should in the future. You know all of us have to follow rules. I have rules to follow, Sheriff Fleming has rules to follow, Bishop Yoder has rules to follow. Just think how terrible it would be if everyone did as they pleased. It would be like a jungle and all the bad people would cause all kinds of trouble for the rest of us."

"I did not think of that. Oh, why is my head hurting so bad?"

"I have an idea, but I need to get your mother's permission to give you some tests. Please sit here in my office. I'm sure your mother will be here quickly. She will be so anxious to see for herself that you're all right."

While Jeremiah was telling Dr. Yoder about how he had spent the two weeks, Charity ran in. She immediately burst into tears and rushed to hug Jeremiah.

"My darling son, I am so glad and happy to see you. Your grandfathers and grandmother and all your uncles and aunts are going to rejoice. We have all been praying so hard. Even people in the church have been having prayer meetings for you." She was so excited that she talked strictly in the Amish language.

Micah beamed at her. Isaac Yoder finally got a word in.

"Charity, I think you need to hear what Micah has to say about Jeremiah. We need to have some serious discussions."

"Oh, Micah. Why? Is he in trouble, other than with me?" She pretended to frown at Jeremiah.

There was a knock on the door. Deputy Glenn had brought Jacob and Joshua back to the hospital. They came hurriedly in and both rushed to take Jeremiah from Charity's arms. They just held him for a few minutes.

"Jeremiah," Jacob spoke, "we love you and have been so worried about your safety. Where did you sleep? How did you eat?"

"Where have you been," Joshua put in. "We looked and looked and no one know where you had gone until the boy that stayed behind said you planned on going to Florida. How did you expect to live?"

Dr. Yoder interrupted. "All of those questions will be answered. I want all of you to hear what Micah has to say about Jeremiah." He stuck his head out of the door. "Nurse Beemer, would you come here, please?"

"Yes, Dr. Yoder. You wanted me?"

"Yes. Would you please take Jeremiah here down for a soft drink and maybe some ice cream?" He wiggled his eyebrows at her to show that he wanted to talk without Jeremiah hearing.

"I shall be delighted. It isn't every day I get such a handsome gentleman to have some free time with. Would you like to come with me, Jeremiah? I know where we can get a delicious sundae. Do you like those?"

"I sure do," Jeremiah was thrilled to get something he hadn't had all the time he had been gone. "See you later," he called over his shoulder as he went happily with the nurse.

Charity was very concerned. "Why all the secrecy, Micah? Did Jeremiah get into trouble of some kind?"

"Not what you're thinking. First I want to tell you what I did the morning we left Fayetteville, North Carolina."

"How did they get down there?" Joshua asked in wonder.

"Maybe I'd better start there," Micah stated. He told them what the boys had told him of stealing, breaking into people's homes, of Morton's temper and destruction of property, of his bullying them, of sleeping out in all kinds of weather and going hungry part of the time. He then told them of being notified that they had been found.

"Why did you not tell us before you left?" Jacob asked.

"I didn't know for sure it was the same boys. I didn't want you to get your hopes up and then be disappointed. Okay, now let me tell you what I did the day we left." He told them how the officers and Judge Stallard cooperated and taught the boys a lesson. "It doesn't matter to me whether you approve of what I did or not, it worked. They were four scared boys who were honestly sorry for what they had done." He laughed, "Besides, they were so glad to get food and be in the dry."

An hour and a half had passed while Micah was reporting. Isaac politely broke in to the conversation.

"I need to speak now. Jeremiah will return soon and I would rather he had hear this yet. Charity, I was suspicious of something before Jeremiah left, but he left too quickly for me to follow up. Now, after today, I am very concerned."

"What?" Charity broke in, "is there something wrong that is life threatening. Why is he complaining of so many headaches?"

"Let me get a chance to explain."

Jacob reached over and placed a hand over Charity's hands that she was wringing together in her lap. She kept quit.

"Thank you. Now I was suspicious of his mood swings and after he ran away, I was almost convinced. However, I have to run some tests to be sure, and I need your permission to do so?"

"What kind of tests? What do you suspect?"

"I suspect a brain tumor. I must take an MRI or a CAT scan."

"What are they!?"

"MRI stand for Magnetic Resonance Imaging which uses special magnets and radio frequency to see deeper than an x-ray can. CAT scan stands for Computerized Tomography scan uses rays and computer technology to show cross sections. This can show bones, muscles, fat and organs. Both of these are more detailed than general x-rays."

"I do not know any more than I did, but I trust you to do the best for my son."

"Thank you. The first clue I had was the personality change and irritability. Now we know headaches and depression."

"Is this cancer?"

"I don't think so. Brain tumors are more common than you might think in children."

Joshua stirred nervously. "What exactly is a brain tumor?"

"Let me give you some ease. Once the tumor is removed it will not come back. A tumor is an abnormal growth of tissue. Cancerous tumors are fast growing and Jeremiah has been exhibiting signs for well over a year. That is why I don't think you have anything to worry about. I can go into more detail, but I don't think it would help you know what is going on in our little guy's head."

Jacob was setting forward in his chair listening intently. "What causes brain tumors?"

"Abnormal cell growth. I personally don't think they're inherited. Sometimes children who have received radiation treatment for something else will develop tumors, but that isn't Jeremiah's case."

"What can you do for him?" Charity asked.

"First I need to run the tests and see what is going on in his brain. Then if we find that it truly is a tumor, I can do surgery. I need your permission for anything and everything," he smiled.

"Where are the papers? I will be glad to sign anything that will help him. How soon can you start?" Charity was eager.

"I'll call a nurse in to bring the necessary papers. Then I'll check the days that the tests are available. The radiologist has to read the tests and send a written report to me. After I consult with him about the tests, we will then schedule whatever what has to be done."

Jeremiah burst in the door happily telling them of eating a banana split. "It is not as good as your cake. Mamm. I can not wait to get home and have you cook for me." Everyone laughed and Jacob reached to bring him to his side for another hug.

"How long will this take?" Joshua asked.

"From one to two weeks. I need time to do what is best for my patient."

Jeremiah looked with concern from one person's face to another. "You have been talking about me. What is going on?"

Charity reached to put her arms around him. "Dr. Yoder is going to run going to tests some tests to see why you are having these bad headaches."

"What kind of tests?" Jeremiah asked with concern.

Dr. Yoder sat down to be near Jeremiah's eyes. "Nothing for you to be afraid of. I will take some big machines and look into your head and brain to find the problem. We'll make you feel much better."

Giving a big sigh Jeremiah said, "I will be thankful for you to do so and will be very glad when it is over."

"You might have to stay in the hospital with me for a long time, but you're a big, strong boy and can take it."

"I sure can," he strutted around the room. "When do we start?"

"I'll be in touch and let you know. Now why don't you go home with your folks and enjoy your mother's good cooking."

"Yeah!" he yelled like any normal boy and headed out the door. Charity, Jacob and Joshua thanked Isaac and left. Deputy Glenn was waiting to take them all home.

CHAPTER EIGHTEEN

Two days later Isaac drove to Charity's house. He was welcomed and offered a piece of Jeremiah's Banana Split cake and a cup of coffee. He sat at the kitchen table to eat and talk to Charity.

"Dr. Yoder," Charity began.

"I told you to call me Isaac."

"Isaac," she smiled, "what news do you have about the tests for Jeremiah?"

"That's why I'm here. I have scheduled the MRI for next Tuesday and the CAT scan for Thursday. It may be overkill, but I want a good, clear picture of what is inside his head."

"I do appreciate it. As you know, we don't carry insurance, but I have enough to pay for whatever he needs. Just make him well, please Gott."

"Don't worry about payment yet. I'll pick him up at eight Tuesday morning and bring him back some time after lunch. I'll make sure he is fed and cared for."

"Do you mean I can not go with him?"

"Charity, you would not be permitted in the room where the tests are taking place, and you would just sit outside and get tired. Why don't you go on to work and keep your mind occupied? Have something to do. Don't you trust me to take good care of him? I care for both of you a great deal."

"Ja. Ja, I trust you. It is just so soon after I lost him for two weeks and I want to be with him as much as possible. Besides, every little child needs their mother with them when they are in the hospital."

"I understand how you feel, and if he were in the hospital, I would say you could sit with him. When he gets there you won't see him at all until the tests are over."

"All right, I will have him ready for you, but we will be at my store. You can pick him up there."

"Fine with me and do you want me to return him there?"

"Please. I will be on pins and needles until I see him and hear from you."

"Charity, I shall not allow you to suffer one minute," he laughed. "I shall be delighted to bring him wherever you want him."

"I can not keep from being concerned. It is my only child and something is wrong in his head. Of course I am worried. I will have him ready for you and grateful that you are such a good friend."

"Charity, I will always be your friend." He started to say more but decided to wait. He meant to remind her of how much she meant to him. He felt the time was not right.

He left and went to his office at the hospital. Charity could hardly wait to talk to her father and father-in-law to tell them the news. She didn't want to say much where Jeremiah could hear because he would not understand all of it and might be frightened.

First she went to talk to Bishop Jonah Slabough, who had taken the place of Amos Yoder who was so sick. She told him of Jeremiah's behavior and what Dr. Yoder wanted to do.

"God gave the skill to the doctors to help us and we would be foolish not to accept them," Jonah assured her.

"We will keep praying for Jeremiah and for you because you have had so much grief and suffering."

"But our Lord has given me more blessings than I can count and I am so thankful," she stated.

"I am so pleased that you give proper credit to our Lord for we could not survive without him and without His mercy."

"Ja. Danki, Bishop. May Gott segeneich." (Yes. Thank you, Bishop. May God bless you.)

"D Herr sei mit du," he answered her as she left. (The Lord be with you.)

Charity got in her buggy and drove to Jacob's house. He was out in his workroom building more beautiful, finished furniture.

"Oh, daed, I thought you were going to do your work at the store."

"I do some, but this is for a neighbor who will pick it up when it is ready. I have a lot to do yet. What is on your mind?"

She proceeded to tell him of the appointments for Jeremiah. He promptly said he was going and she had to explain why she could not even go. He promised to tell Joshua and Leah and she went back home. Jeremiah would be home from school soon. He would probably have to repeat the sixth year, but that didn't bother her.

She went home planning what she would provide for the Sunday service. This Sunday it would be at the home of Bishop Slabough. She would go over on Saturday and offer to help with any housework or extra cooking.

Sunday rolled around cold but clear. A huge crowd had gathered for this service for they were going to discuss some business as well as have a worship service. Charity had baked a ham with vegetables around it, potato salad and a cake. Jeremiah was unusually quiet and thoughtful.

"What are you thinking, Jeremiah," she asked as she guided her horse through the crowd of buggies.

"Nothing special, mamm. I am just wondering where Morty is and if the police found him. They said because of his age and all he had done that he would probably go to jail. I am so thankful I did not have to go. Those two nights I spent in the cell were scary. Drunks were yelling and threatening the guards and the guards were cursing them and beating on the cell bars with a stick."

"I am so sorry you had that experience, but maybe God allowed you to have it so you would not get into real serious trouble later."

"I guess you are right. Mamm, when can I drive the horse? Grossvader Joshua took my horse away for a while. I do not know when I will get him back. This time I will listen carefully and do as I am told. I want to be a good horseman like my daed."

"Your daed was the best and he treated all animals with love and respect. He did not rush his training or beat them. He would be so proud of you now."

"He would not be proud of what I did by leaving with those older boys and getting into trouble."

"No, his heart would be broken, but you will not do anything like that again, will you."

"No, mamm, I sure will not. Oh, my head hurts so bad. What is wrong with me?"

"Dr. Yoder has scheduled your tests for this week and we will soon know. Try to be brave and ask God to protect you."

Much to Charity's embarrassment the business was about Jeremiah's coming tests and the cost involved. The Bishop was asking people to contribute more to the benevolent fund. He also asked for volunteers to do her chores while her son was in the hospital.

Charity stood quickly. She heard gasps around her because women did not, as a rule, speak out in business meeting or in worship services.

"Bishop Slabough, may I have permission to speak?"

"Yes, my child. What is it you want to say?"

"I love all of my brothers and sisters as God wants us to. I will not have to stay in the hospital and can take care of my chores with my brudders' help. I am sure that I can make enough money in the store to pay the costs. Please use our fund to help someone who is desperately in need such as a fire or an accident. Thank you all for your love and caring, but with God's help, I will be all right. Please continue to pray for Jeremiah."

Jeremiah was embarrassed at being in the spotlight, but he sat quietly and straight-backed as he was taught.

With the business meeting, the service took three and a half hours. The people were more than ready for lunch. The men quickly converted the benches into tables and the women hurried to bring out the food. The teenage girls passed beverages to everyone and the younger girls passed bread. The boys would help clean up after the meal, pick up the benches and load them on the wagon to be used a the next service, while the men talked and the women took care of left-over food.

On the way home Jeremiah wanted to know more about his tests. Charity could understand that he was nervous.

"Dr. Yoder will let you see the machines and explain everything to you when you go to the hospital. He can do a better job than I can do. It might be a little uncomfortable, but it will not be painful and nothing will hurt you."

"I will be brave. I am so glad I am not running and hiding while feeling so dirty and hungry and scared. I can take anything Dr. Yoder wishes to do."

"I know you can. You are my young man and, even though you broke my heart for a short time and I was so worried, I love you so much and am proud of you."

"Thank you, mamm. I will always try to make you proud."

On Monday Isaac came to the house to talk to Jeremiah. He had pictures of the machines and showed him how they worked. "There will be some banging noises in the tube for the MRI, but nothing will hurt you. In fact, sometimes they have earphones that play music while you are in there and you will pay no attention to the banging. It will take almost an hour, so you must be brave and lie very still."

"I will, Dr. Yoder. I will be very brave. Do you think my dad and grandmother will look down and see me?"

"I don't know about that, but I do know your guardian angel will be with you and God never leaves us. You will be well cared for."

"I will be happy to have anything that will take away these headaches and awful feeling. I am sorry that it made me do bad thing."

"That's all in the past. Think about the future and what great plans you're going to make. I'll pick you up at eight tomorrow morning."

"Thank you. I will get up early and do my chores and be ready."

Jeremiah was waiting impatiently for Dr. Yoder. Charity was so anxious and sad that she could not go and hold her son while the tests were being made. She would go on to the store and try to stay busy to keep from thinking too much.

"Mamm, here is Dr. Yoder. Look! I will get to ride in his big car. We will go fast and be there in a short time."

Jeremiah ran out before Charity could get to the door. She stepped out to thank Isaac again and say she would be anxious to know the results.

"We won't know anything today, Charity. A radiologist has to read the report and then send it to the doctor. We'll more than likely wait until the CAT scan to put it all together. I probably won't be able to tell you anything until the first of next week."

"Oh, I did so hope we would know today," Charity said.

"I'm sorry, but it doesn't work that quickly. I'll take good care of our boy and feed him before I bring him back to you this afternoon."

"Thank you again. Bye Jeremiah." Charity kept repeating Psalm 55:22, *Cast your cares on the Lord and He will sustain you.*

She went on to the store with a heavy heart, but soon was too busy to do much thinking. Seven Amish women had come in to quilt. Two Amish women and three English women were making clothing for the English who had placed orders. A lot of tourists came in and all of them bought something.

Charity had her back to the door when a friendly voice called out, "Hello everyone."

She whirled around and gaped in surprise. She was quickly hugged by Bonnie Kate Mercer and Emily Hutchinson. Their husbands Bernard Mercer and Bill Hutchinson just smiled at her.

"I'm so sorry we didn't get back sooner, although I did send several friends to you. One of my friends bought a complete set of bedroom furniture and she is thrilled." Bonnie Kate was so happy to be back that she had trouble stopping incessant talking. Bernard put an arm around her.

"Hold on, sweetheart. We're all glad to be here. What Bonnie has not told you is that a month, or so, after we were here I fell off a ladder, where I was cleaning out the gutters, and broke my hip. I was unable to travel for a long time. Then we got pregnant and Bonnie gave birth to a downs syndrome girl. We have been in and out of hospitals with her, but we lost her at three years of age. We've neither one had any interest in traveling."

"I am so sorry. I do not know what to say," Charity felt like crying. "It is so unfair to want a child as much as you did and then to lose her. I would not be able to go on living if anything happened to Jeremiah."

Emily held up an antique pie press. "How much do you want for this? My mother would love to have it."

"I have not put a price on it yet because I was not sure what to charge. Let me ask someone and I will let you know."

"While the ladies are doing all the talking, I would like to ask about your son," Bill spoke up quickly.

"Oh, you have been gone a long time. He will be ten soon and he has been a handful. He got into some trouble which helped him learn a valuable lesson and he is now my sweet son again. He is having MRIs and CAT scans to determine why he is having so many headaches and why his personality changed so much."

"Charity, it sounds as if you, too, have had some heartaches. Forgive us for barging in and sounding so happy, but we are happy to see you again."

Bonnie Kate assured her.

"Yes, my mother died from cancer and my father keeps going but I know deep in his heart he is hurting. They were married at a young age and have been in love since they were children."

"I'm sorry," Emily said. "We barged in here bringing joy and you have had so much to bear."

"I have not had any more than others, and the Lord takes care of us. We do not always understand why His will is so upsetting to us, but He loves us and cares about us."

At that time Jeremiah burst in the door talking as he came. "Oh, mamm, you would not believe the big machine I was in. They put me on a table and then the table slid back into a big tube and wow! What banging. It was wonderful. I did get tired of having to be so still, but it is fine. Dr. Yoder took me to the hospital cafeteria and we had the best lunch and then an ice cream sundae."

"Holy Hannah. This tall, good-looking young man can't be Jeremiah."

Bonnie Kate was surprised.

He turned looking quizzically at her. "Yes, I am Jeremiah. Who are you?"

"Jeremiah, do not be rude. This is the good doctor who took care of you when you were just a baby and a spider bit you."

"Yes, you have told me about them. Thank you, and thank you for the money you left. My mother put it in the bank and has been adding to it, but I can not get it until I am twenty-five."

Everyone laughed. Bernard stood next to Jeremiah and placed a hand on his shoulder. "We are so glad you are doing well. I hear you're an honor student. What work would you like to do when you complete your education?"

"I have been thinking, and I think I would like to be a doctor like Dr. Yoder and help children get well."

Isaac chuckled. "Jeremiah, you have no idea how many years of school you would need or how hard you would have to work. It's not so glamorous when you are working with someone and trying you best and they die in spite of all you can do."

Charity chuckled. "You have two more years of schooling in your Amish classes. We will talk then about what you want to do." Looking at her guests she invited, "Please come with me and have a seat. We will have some pastries. Would you like hot cider, coffee, water, milk or a soft drink?" She called to Rebeka Bergerstein to serve them.

Bill did his best to suck in his stomach. "I need pastries like I need a hole in my head, but the odors are mouth-watering. I'll join you. I'd like to try some hot cider. Thank you."

As they walked through the store the four exclaimed at the addition of rooms and all that was offered. They spoke pleasantly to workers and volunteers as they went back.

Charity seated them at one of the bigger tables joined by Jeremiah and Isaac Yoder. Charity sent for Rosemary to join them telling her guests how much she depended on Rosemary and what she had done to help. Rosemary was embarrassed but secretly pleased that Charity appreciated her so much. They had been friends since early childhood.

With interruptions from Jeremiah, Isaac and Rosemary, Charity told them of her trip to Shipshewana and her attackers. She and Rosemary told of the men coming to Shickshinny and trying to rob a jewelry store. Charity then told of one man being in her store of meeting U. S. Marshal Richard Longbow.

This took so long that Isaac had to run to get back to the hospital.

Jeremiah hung his head and said, "As long as stories are being told, I might as well tell you what mamm meant by me being in trouble."

Charity looked at him with pride and tears in her eyes as she realized that Jeremiah was maturing after all. He could face what he had done, but she was sure he would not give her any more trouble.

They were surprised that four hours had gone by, and everyone had left the store. The girls, working for Charity, had checked everything and closed up.

Charity was so happy to see them that she invited them to her house for supper.

"Charity," Emily and Bonnie Kate began at the same time. They laughed. Emily continued. "We would love to see your home and spend more time with you and Jeremiah, but we have reservations at a B&B and want to do more sightseeing."

"Maybe we can return on another day, at a better time, and spend more time with you. We would love to have you come see us, also," Bonnie Kate said as she stood and twisted around to get her back straightened.

The two men thanked her for her hospitality and the delicious food. Bill and Bernard had stood talking quietly to each other in another part of the room. They came to Jeremiah. Bernard said, "Jeremiah, we are so proud of you for becoming an excellent student and a wonderful gentleman. We are going to give you something that your mother will possibly not like, but we want to do it. Bill and I are giving you one hundred dollars to put into that bank account. It will grow and maybe pay for an education that will help you achieve your desires."

Jeremiah did not know what to say. He looked hopefully at his mother. She was undecided and wondered what her father would say. She finally nodded and Jeremiah accepted the money with a big grin.

"Thank you. Yes, I will put it in the bank and I want to go on to school past what we have here. The Bishop will have to approve, but I do not think he will object when he hears what I would like to do."

With hugs all around and promises to keep in touch, the four left to continue their vacation. Lawrence had driven to take Charity and Jeremiah home. Jeremiah talked his ears off telling him about the visitors and his test that day.

Charity was gratified to learn that Lawrence and Joseph had done the chores. She only had to get supper. She invited Lawrence to stay, but he declined.

Jeremiah wanted egg sandwiches, so she made bacon and fried egg sandwiches with hot apples and potato salad on the side. Jeremiah had milk and Charity had hot peppermint tea.

Jeremiah read the Bible passages and they had prayer together. They each went to their own room, dressed for the night and thankfully got onto a soft, comfortable feather mattress.

Wednesday passed and then Charity had to get Jeremiah up Thursday morning for his CAT scan. Dr. Yoder picked him up promptly at eight and told Charity that this would not take as long.

Jeremiah was delivered to her in time for them to have lunch together. Now she had to wait impatiently for the results of the test. She didn't hear anything from Isaac until Monday afternoon of the following week.

Jeremiah was at school, but Charity was at the store. He asked her to go sit in his car with him so they could talk privately. She was worried because Isaac looked very serious.

"Please, Isaac, tell me if my son will live, and can you do anything to help him?"

"Yes and yes. Jeremiah had a small tumor of his brain. That will have to come out. He has had pressure on his brain. I'm more concerned about all the fluid I found. That must be drained off."

"How did he get a tumor and what do you mean by fluid on the brain?"

"I could give you a lot of medical vocabulary which you would not understand. I'll try to tell you as simply as I can. If it is the tumor I'm thinking about it is called an astrocytomas which comes from connective tissue cells called astrocytes. It is the most common type of brain tumors in children. We can remove it easily as it is still in the formation stages. Headaches and vomiting are the most common side effects. It can be malignant if not treated. Jeremiah's has been diagnosed in time."

"I only understood part of that. The most important is that Jeremiah is not in immediate danger, or is not going to die."

"No, Charity, he will not die. I'll see to that. Now to the fluid. I need to do a biopsy to be sure of my findings about the type of tumor. The fluid is sometimes found on infants. Tumors occur in the very young, but most of them are six years old before becoming affected."

"Isaac, is this something new like polio?"

"No, it is not new and there might have been polio in ancient Egypt. Information regarding fluid on the brain has been found in ancient Egyptian medical scrolls from 2500 BC. The ancient Greek physician, Hippocrates, wrote of it in the fourth century BC. A more enlightening description was written by the Roman physician, Galen, in the second century AD. The most informative surgical descriptions come from an Arab surgeon, Abulcasis."

"All of that is real Greek to me," Charity laughed.

"Water, or fluid, on the brain is abnormal accumulation of cerebrospinal fluid (CSF)."

"Stop, stop, Isaac. I don't know any more than I did. I am just so anxious to know all that I can about my son's problems. Will any of this come back later?"

"I seriously doubt that it will. There really isn't much fluid and the tumor is still small. I want to do a biopsy tomorrow and keep him in the hospital. With your permission, after the biopsy is diagnosed, I would like to proceed with the surgery."

"Isaac, you know you have my permission. Will you be doing the surgery?"

"Usually Dr. David Boggs works on the children, but I'm sure he won't be offended if I request to do the surgery on Jeremiah."

"Is that all you can tell me now?"

"Yes, as of today, but I promise to keep you informed."

Chapter Nineteen

Charity awakened on Tuesday morning feeling discombobulated. She was worried about Jeremiah having the surgery and yet she knew it was necessary. Trying to shake the amorphous thoughts she took a shower and dressed to go do her chores.

She was thankful to see Joseph had already arrived and started the work. She could not talk and only hugged him. He understood because she had told them that the work on Jeremiah would start today.

Jeremiah was not going to be happy. He had to go in without eating. She knew he was concerned about the whole process, and felt helpless that she could not tell him more and relieve him of his anxiety.

Jeremiah was up and dressed just in time for Isaac to pick him up at six thirty. Joseph and Charity did not tell him good bye. They reminded him that they loved him and that God loved him. His guardian angel would be with him all through the surgery. He left with a smile on his face. Charity fell against Joseph crying. He hugged her and comforted her the best he could.

Jeremiah was given a relaxant and finally went to sleep. His head was completely shaved and the tiny cut was made for the biopsy. Isaac hurried the decision through as to what kind of tumor it was. The results came back that afternoon and he was right. It was benign. He scheduled the drainage of the fluid for the following morning. On Thursday he would do the surgery and remove the tumor. He, too, prayed that all would go well.

On Friday Jeremiah opened his eyes and felt of a bandage covering his head like a shower cap. He didn't feel badly at all; in fact he was quite pleased with himself.

A nurse came in and asked him if he was ready to eat. He felt hollow and almost shouted at her to bring on the food. After he had eaten a scrambled egg, a croissant, a slice of honey dew melon and a glass of milk, he felt full.

The nurse called for another nurse to help her. Jeremiah was embarrassed that they bathed him, changed his bedding and put him back in bed.

He thanked them as he had been taught. Much to his chagrin he fell asleep.

He woke much later feeling someone rubbing his arm. He looked up into the smiling eyes of his mother.

"Mamm! I am so glad to see you. Look at my head."

"I have been looking. You are still very handsome. Your hair will grow quicker than you think. Before long this will just be a memory. How do you feel?"

"I am super. When can I go home?"

"You will have to be in here for a few days so that Dr. Yoder can make sure you are well and strong again."

"But I am strong. See." He bent his arm to show his mother his biceps.

"I am glad to see you still have good muscle. We have a lot of work to do when you get back home."

"Oh," he said disgustedly. Then he perked up. "Now that I am better and behaving do you think the grossfaders will let me have my horse back? I will promise to do all they tell me and work hard."

"I am sure they will be so pleased to hear that. You will have to talk to them about getting the horse back. You will have to prove yourself."

"I can do that, mamm. I promise I can."

"I am sure you can, but you will have to convince your grandfathers."

Dr. David Boggs came into the room. "Well, how is our star patient today? You came through the surgery like a trooper. Hello, are you his mother?"

Charity introduced herself and thanked him for the excellent care Jeremiah was receiving. Dr. Boggs did the checking on stats and wrote on the chart at the foot of the bed.

"It was nice meeting you," he told Charity. "And you, young man, keep doing as well as you are and you'll be home in a short time. Have a nice day." He hurried out with his white coat flying behind him.

"Mamm, I like being in the hospital because they do take good care of me, but I love being at home with you more."

"I am glad you like being at home. I missed you so much when you decided to leave home. I worried every day and most of every night. I could not sleep or eat and was so distressed."

"I am so sorry that I made you worry, but it will never happen again."

Isaac came in and greeted them as if they were long-lost relatives. "Hey, buddy boy. How is my favorite patient?"

"Fine, can I go home?" Jeremiah almost yelled he was so happy.

"You'll need to stay here for a few days. You're feeling good now, but when the medication wears off, you might feel differently."

"No, I will not. Let me go home with my mamm, today, puhleeese."

"Sorry. No can do. Let's see what's written on your chart." He read and then turned to Charity with a smile. "Looks as if everything is going well.

I need to talk to you. Would you mind stepping outside to the waiting room?"

"Are you going to talk about me and do not want me to hear it?" Jeremiah pouted.

"No, friend. Not all conversations are about you. Lie back and rest. You'll need it to heal quickly and go home."

Isaac led Charity to an office and shut the door. "Would you like some coffee or something to nibble on?"

"Nee, danki." She was so nervous she lapsed into Amish. "Are you going to give me bad news about Jeremiah?"

"No. Jeremiah is doing well. We are fortunate to have caught this in time. I need to talk to you about your own health. I don't want to upset you, but remember your mother would not come in for regular check-ups and you lost her. Jeremiah only sees a doctor when he is already sick. If your mother had been coming in, the doctors would have caught the cancer and been able to treat her. You are lucky that Jeremiah's symptoms led us to suspect his problem and we were able to help him. All of you must develop a regular check-up with some doctor, not necessarily me, although I would love to help. I would like to schedule you for a check-up and make sure you have nothing that can be disastrous. It would devastate Jeremiah to give up his mother. The two of you are very close. What do you say?"

Charity was silent for a moment. "Ja, I will make an appointment for a check-up and I will talk to my relatives and tell them what you have told me. It does make sense. We Amish depend on ourselves and home medicines for most illnesses, but I can understand about something we do not know about. I will talk to them."

Monday, of the following week, Jeremiah was allowed to go home with the understanding that a Home Health care nurse would check on him and change his bandage as needed. By the end of the week the bandage came off for good. The stitches would come out in another week.

He was jubilant and had to be reminded often to not be so exuberant.

He was deliriously happy to get his horse back and resume riding lessons. It did not bother him that he would have to take the sixth year over. School was now out for the summer and he was looking forward to lots of fun. He had several Amish friends and a few nice English friends who came with him.

The boys swam in the river back of the Kime property and ate lunches that loving mothers packed for them. All of them had their own horse and were allowed to go on a trail ride in the mountains with two or three adults going with them.

They camped out a couple of nights and sang around a campfire. Tracy Goodson's daddy told ghost stories. Michael and Lawrence told them stories of when they were little boys. There was still no news of Morton Richardson. Was he alive or dead, or was he even still in this country?

They learned how to dig a hole and pile the dirt and rocks around the outside to make a fire pit. Then when they were ready to leave the dirt was put on the embers to make sure a forest fire would not start. They had a wonderful summer and were ready for school to begin.

TWENTY YEARS LATER

Jacob, Joshua and Leah were beside Jenna Mae in the Amish cemetery.

Indiana University of Pennsylvania

The audience moved restlessly with anticipation. Charity was there with her husband, Isaac Yoder. They had four-year-old twins, Jacob and Jenna.

Michael was now a grandfather and was there with his entire brood. Lawrence was present with all nine of his children, some engaged to be married. Maeve and her husband were holding a new born. Alicia was sitting with Charity. She had never married and was living with Charity to help her with house, children and store.

Joseph had broken Amish tradition and joined the U.S. Marines. He could not attend because he was on duty, but his wife and two children were present. Joseph had sent a telegram of congratulations and was eager to get home and see the family.

Bonnie Kate Mercer was now a widow, but she was present with some friends. It seemed that the majority of Shickshinny had traveled here today to give honor to one of their own. Richard Longbow, retired, was present with his wife and three children.

Amid applause, the President came out and gave a short speech. He said, "And now let me introduce you to your new doctors whom, I am sure, will be worthy of the title."

He started with the last names beginning with A. When he came to Doctor Jeremiah Adam Kime, it seemed that half the audience stood up and cheered. Charity had happy tears in her eyes. Isaac quietly wiped his eyes for he loved this now dear son of his.

Jeremiah, too, had promised the Bishop if he were permitted to continue his education that he would come back and work at least five years in his community. It was an Amish Promise he intended to keep.

AUTHOR'S NOTE

DAS LOBLIED

This is a hymn of praise sung slowly. I am told that to sing the entire song takes fifteen minutes. I hope I've spelled all correctly. I can't put in the punctuation marks over the words. There are fifteen verses.

O Gott Vader, wir loben dich und deine Guete preisen:
Das du, Dich o Herr, gnadiglidh un uns neu hast beweisen,
Und hast uns Herr zusammen g'fuhrt, uns zu ermahnen durch Dein Wort,
Gieb uns Genad zu diesem

O Lord Father, we bless thy name, thy love and thy goodness praise:
That Thou, O Lord, so graciously have been with us always.
Thou hast brought us together, O Lord, to be admonished through Thy word.
Bestow on us Thy grace.

****

The young people gather on Sunday night to sing usually where the church service was held that morning. They are given refreshments. They may play volleyball or touch and go (tag). They sing spirituals and some country music. They love Johnny Cash and spirituals by country singers. Harmonicas or mouth organs are allowed.

****

Amish children are sung to all the time. Sometimes a child's song or a church song that the parent especially likes. The babies hear a song like our "Ride a Horse to Branberry Cross". They are trotted on the knees and then bounced at the end.

Rad-dy, rad-dy gal-ly halbst und de mayle mai-a mus-sa ma ha-ve dres-sa
Fas gal-la fud-da fres-sa no gam-ma iv-a da barich und de branch barecht run-na

Ridey, ridey horsie half an hour a mile. Tomorrow we have to thrash oats for horsie to eat food. Then we go over the bridge and the bridge breaks down.

The older youngsters sing a song to the tune of "Twinkle, Twinkle Little Star".

In der stillen einsamkeit findest du mein lob bereit
Grosser Gott erhore mich denn mein herze suche dich

In the still isolation You find my praise ready
Greater God hear me for my heart is seeking You

There are four verses to this, but I have only provided the first verse of each.

SOME TASTY TREATS TO ENJOY FROM SIOUX DALLAS

Banana Split Cake
Low calories, easy to prepare and liked by all. No baking.
9 whole fat-reduced graham crackers
1 large sugar-free vanilla pudding (can use instant pudding or pie filling mix)
3 cups skim milk
3 medium ripe bananas (sliced)
2 cups fat-free whipped topping
1 full cup strawberries (sliced)
2 cups crushed pineapple (drained)

Place the graham crackers on the bottom of a 9" x 13" pan. Mix the pudding with the skim milk. Spread this layer over the graham crackers. Spread the drained pineapples over this layer. Slice 2 bananas and lay them over this layer. Spread the sliced strawberries over this. Slice the third banana over the top. Optional to add nuts. Cover with whipped topping and place in refrigerator to chill.

Fruit Slush

Favorite of the Amish children. (Remember they squeeze fruit and can by hand.)
12 ounces frozen orange juice
20 ounce can of crushed pineapple with juice
1 quart sliced peaches
8 mashed bananas
1 cup sugar (May use Splenda)

Mix orange juice with 1 cup water. Mix with remaining ingredients. Place in pitchers and freeze. May eat with spoon or drink partially frozen

Corn Fritters

2 cups fresh corn (or canned) whole kernel
2 eggs beaten
One-fourth cup flour
1 teaspoon salt -- dash of pepper
1 teaspoon baking powder
2 tablespoons cream
4 tablespoons low fat oil or margarine (melted)

Combine eggs, flour, baking powder, corn and salt and pepper to taste. Mix thoroughly. Add cream. Melt margarine in hot skillet. Drop tablespoons in on hot skillet, flatten slightly. Brown on both sides. Serve as is or with syrup.

Amish Delicious Soft Pretzels

Preheat oven to 550 degrees
One and one-fourth cup warm water (105 degrees)
1 tablespoon active yeast
One-fourth cup brown sugar
2 cups flour

Melt sweet creamy butter for dipping pretzels. May use sea salt. Dissolve yeast in water. Mix well. Add sugar. Mix. Add flour, but do not knead as it will make the dough tough. Let rise, covering with white cloth until doubled.

Cut into long ropes. Shape ropes into pretzel. Dip in melted butter. Place on well-greased cookie sheet and sprinkle with sea salt. Bake for 4 to 6 <u>minutes</u> until golden brown

Spritz Cookies

Two and one-half cup all-purpose flour
One-half teaspoon salt
Three-fourths teaspoon ground cinnamon
1 cup sugar
2 egg yolks (or one large egg)
2 teaspoons vanilla extract
1 cup softened butter

Preheat oven to 375 degrees. Combine butter, vanilla and egg yolks beating on high speed until fluffy and light. Add sugar and mix until sugar is dissolved. In another bowl whisk flour, salt and cinnamon. Add to butter mixture and barely mix. Drop from tablespoon on ungreased baking sheet leaving at least one inch between. Bake until lightly browned for 10 to 12 <u>minutes</u>. If you have a cookie press, it is easier to drop cookies. May use sprinkles, colored sugar or mini-chocolate chips for topping.

Granola Bars

Preheat oven to 325 degrees. Line 15" x 10" inch pan with foil and grease
One-half cup melted butter
2 teaspoons ground cinnamon
One and one-half cup raw old-fashioned oats
One and one-half cup quick one minute oats (raw)
One and one-half cup peanuts (use any favorite nut)
1 cup sunflower seeds
1 cup raisins
1 (14 oz.) can Eagle Brand Sweetened Condensed
    Milk (not evaporated)

Mix all ingredients one at a time stirring well. Pour into pan and press down with buttered hands. Bake until golden brown, usually 30 minutes. Cut into bars and store at room temperature.

Amish Haystack

1 large head of lettuce (washed) broken up
4 tomatoes diced
1 onion diced
1 large bag of crushed taco chips
3 pounds fried, seasoned to taste, hamburger
1 cup diced hard boiled eggs
1 pound crushed no salt soda crackers
2 cups hot, but uncooked, rice
4 cans Campbell's cheese soup (add milk as
    directed and heat)
1 package crushed pecans
1 container sour cream

Place each item in layers as listed and top with the cheese sauce (cheese & milk).

These recipes are so popular with the Amish, that they serve these at fundraisers and are successful. I hope you will enjoy these recipes. Add them to the ones in *Amish Dilemma*.

Some of you have questioned my making stuffing and dressing being separate.

My stuffing is made of Jimmy Dean Sage sausage, hazelnuts, diced celery and anything else you want to use. I stuff this in the turkey the morning that I am going to bake it. Take it out with a tablespoon and pour gravy over it.

My dressing is an old recipe handed down from generation to generation.

Use at least one quart of broth (either turkey or chicken). I often buy the cans of chicken broth. Add 2 or 3 eggs and mix well. Season to taste and add enough salt-free soda crackers to make a paste. Don't get it too dry or it will not taste as well as moist. Bake in a (cast iron) skillet at 450 degrees (usually 20 to 30 minutes) until golden brown. Cut into slices like pie and pour the gravy over it. I love to make the dressing and just eat it alone.

My mother tried oysters one Thanksgiving with her stuffing. We did not like it.

I love oysters, but not in stuffing.

Also we make a punch of grape juice and a good brand of Ginger Ale. You can float a ring of lime ice cream in this in a punch bowl if you wish.

*Thank God for the Internet. Now that I'm in a wheelchair, I can't go traveling and collecting information as I used to do. Also a heartfelt thank you to my friends who shared recipes and didn't want their names mentioned. The Amish I met and visited in Pennsylvania and the Yoder family here in Florida have been so kind to share and give information.